CW01081021

A Scottish Affair

By H. V. Williams

© Registered 2020 Holly Williams

All rights reserved. No part of this publication may be reproduced, distributed, or transmitted in any form or by any means, including photocopying, recording, or other electronic or mechanical methods, without the prior written permission of the publisher, except in the case of brief quotations embodied in critical reviews and certain other noncommercial uses permitted by copyright law.

Printed in the United States of America by KDP Publishing.

Disclaimer: All persons, events and locations in this book are fictional, or loosely based on actual locations the author has visited. Any likeness to a person or location are mere coincidences.

1.

The scent of warm coffee drifted through the air of the small coffee shop as Charlotte sat sipping hot cappuccino, while looking out of the large window. It was her first time in Edinburgh, having registered at the last minute to attend a conference in the capitol, and she was excited to finally be out of the bustle of downtown Seattle and into the peaceful Scottish city. So far, even though she was exhausted from the long flight over here, she thought the city, and the country, were just breathtaking.

As soon as she got into the city and looked around, she was awed by its beauty and had an unexplainable sense of belonging. Cupping her warm coffee mug, she gazed out of the window at passersby, wondering how many of them were also here for the conference. The sight of people going about their business was comforting to Charlotte, and as she watched couples stop to look in windows, or gently rushing to run errands or to meet commitments, she found herself relishing in the lone time she had to relax and just be.

Working at Seattle University full time while studying to complete her MBA left little time for her to just sit and relax and to embrace the world around her. After she graduated, Charlotte made the decision that she would take time to herself, but her boss made sure that she never really got much time to do anything but sleep and eat. All that overtime and Charlotte still felt that her career was stagnating, but this conference was going to give her the push she needed to change that.

Charlotte didn't often attend conferences, but her University had a last minute opening for her to learn about academic challenges, and with the new software her department was looking to implement, this would be her chance to finally prove that she was capable of leading a team on her own, without Aiden looking over her shoulder at every task. Aiden. What a mistake that had been, she thought to herself, vowing to never again mix business with pleasure.

Back in Seattle, Aiden had given her the chance to work for the University while she finished her MBA. Mainly she completed admin work for the department heads, but under his guidance, she'd found the confidence to apply for a promotion that would allow her to lead her own team. Like most things in Charlotte's life though, it wasn't going to be that easy, first she had to prove that she had what it took to lead, and right now she was in a trial period to do just that. She had hoped that she would be able to use her degree to her advantage, but when things went sour with Aiden, she found a whole new set of professional obstacles that she had to overcome, especially since he was in the Dean's ear all the time. If only she hadn't allowed herself to cross that line from business to casual, maybe then she wouldn't have to be proving herself time and time again.

As she finished her cappuccino, Charlotte's gaze fell to the inside of the coffee shop and to the people who shared the space with her. There were mainly middle-aged businessmen furiously clicking away on their laptops, dotted amongst young couples on first dates and little old ladies looking lovingly at their purchases. The shop was small, but the insides felt so welcoming, from the quaint countertops, filled with delicious looking pastries and cakes, to the antique chalkboards lining the back wall, behind the cash register, and the aromas that filled the air, from sweet sugary treats to that familiar scent of freshly brewed coffee.

The sound of the coffee machine whirring into life as the barista frothed up milk snapped Charlotte back to life. Her own coffee was down to the last dregs and had long since cooled. Looking at the oversized cafe clock on the wall, Charlotte noticed she was now able to check into her hotel. Quickly checking her phone one last time to make sure she had her reservation ready, she jumped up from her spot in the window, just in time to bump head-first into something hard and warm. Looking up, embarrassed, she came face to face to the most beautiful man she had ever seen, much taller than her 5'8 stature, with strong arms that were stopping her from falling over, and almost black hair. Peering into deep blue eyes, so deep she felt that she might fall into them, Charlotte realized she was staring. Excusing herself, and apologizing, she finally righted herself, and released herself from his arms.

"...I'm so sorry, I wasn't paying attention.' She flustered.
"It's ok lass, I got you." He whispered, with a gentle Scottish accent.

Callum couldn't quite get his breath. As he locked eyes with the woman that had just ploughed straight into him, about to be slightly annoyed, he couldn't help but smile. He'd been heading to a seat in the back of the coffee shop while he waited for his black coffee to be made, when she jumped out at him and he caught her. He couldn't ignore the way she felt beneath him, her lithe, yet curvaceous figure, her long, flowing, brown hair, and then those round, deep brown eyes, had him unable to speak for a second. After a minute he noticed she was staring up at him, before she seemed to check herself as her cheeks reddened. She was beautiful. Before he could say more, she was gone.

....

Pulling along her suitcase Charlotte hurried out of the coffee shop, more flustered than she had been in a long time. She rushed to find a taxi to take her to the hotel, though she was sure it was probably within walking distance, she hated to get lost with her luggage.

She managed to flag down an old-fashioned black cab and utter the name of the hotel she was staying at. Climbing into the taxi, she glanced back at the coffee shop to see the handsome stranger she had just bumped into gazing at her through the window. Once again heat filled her cheeks as she bit her lip and hurried into the back seat of the taxi.

By the time she reached the hotel, she was ready to take a nap. It had been a long flight to get here and even the coffee didn't help to alleviate the fatigue tugging at her eyes. Listening to her heels clacking against the hard tile of the hotel lobby, she tried to keep her eyes open as she checked in, got her key, and made her way to the elevator to her room. As she pulled her key card from her wallet, she felt a sense of excitement for what the conference had in store for her, and the experiences she would have while she stayed in Edinburgh.

Though the conference itself would only last for the next four days, Charlotte had decided to take a much needed break, and would be staying in the city for three weeks. She'd chosen a hotel that was right in the heart of Edinburgh so that she was a short walk away from everything the city had to offer, though the conference center was a ten-minute taxi ride away.

Dragging her suitcase into the room, she quietly shut the door, slid off her boots, and lay fully clothed on the bed. She thought a nap sounded great, after that she would take a look at the conference details and make sure she would have everything she needed for the next day.

....

As Callum finished up his second coffee, he couldn't shake the image of the woman who had bumped into him an hour ago. She was so beautiful, and definitely not from around here, he would have remembered seeing her before. Pushing her image from his mind for what seemed like the hundredth time, he refocused on his laptop.

This was the first conference presentation he had put together, and although he was usually cool, calm and collected, something about this conference had him feeling nervous. Given that he was now six years into being a professor at the University of Edinburgh, Callum was used to presenting in front of an audience, so he tried his best to shake off the feeling that this particular conference was any different than his usual day teaching literature to undergraduates.

Callum was an Edinburgh native, having lived in the city his entire life, but after traveling the world a few times over, he'd realized this was the place he wanted to stay for the rest of his life, and that's what made him recently buy his flat in the city center. It was such a great location to be able to be in the heart of Edinburgh and just a short walk from all the attractions, eateries and coffee shops. Still, he'd had to give up his beloved VW Beetle when he last traveled, so now to get to work he had to rely on public transport and ride shares.

Saving his presentation and vowing not to make any more changes, he put away his laptop and stared out the window to take in the city before he made his way home. This coffee shop always helped him to think, people watching helped him to relax and gain perspective before settling in to work on his laptop on most days when he wasn't teaching. Today was like any other, he'd had a class in the morning but decided to come to the coffee shop to finish off his conference presentation, mainly because his presentation happened to be the first one in the morning.

Staring out of the window he watched the bustle of the people in the city, making their way out to dinner or for drinks. He smiled to himself and let his mind wander. Suddenly, the image of the woman who bumped into him came whirling back into his mind. Why couldn't he shake her image? Sure, it wasn't every day that you got bumped into, but it was common enough to not give him this reaction. He put it down to being tired after a long day and decided to take one more look at his laptop.

Callum made a point to check the start time of the conference before putting his laptop away for the second time and gathered his things to make his way to the flat. No more edits, he thought, the presentation will have to stay how it is.

....

2.

*beep**beep**beep*

"What the heck?!" Charlotte had no idea where she was, or what that awful noise was.

*beep**beep**beep*

Slowly, Charlotte opened her eyes and looked around and realization hit. She wasn't in Seattle; she was in Edinburgh! She jumped up and hit the alarm off on the bedside table. Turning on the light, she finally woke up and realized she'd fallen asleep in her clothes as soon as she'd checked into the hotel from the coffee shop, and without the foresight to set the alarm, she was already late for the start of the conference.

"I can't go like this!" she thought. Peeling her clothes off as she hurried to the shower, Charlotte stepped into the warm jet of water and felt her stress levels begin to momentarily ease. She quickly washed herself, taking care not to get her hair too wet and jumped back out of the shower as quickly as she could. Brushing her teeth as she combed her hair, she managed to get dressed and ready in record time. She took one last look in the bathroom mirror.

"Yikes!" quickly coating her eyelashes in mascara and swiping on a thin layer of colored lip gloss, Charlotte made her way out of the hotel room. There were a line of taxi cabs waiting outside of the hotel to take guests on their way, so she grabbed the first one and headed toward the conference center. As her stomach began to growl, she remembered she had a granola bar sitting in her bag from the airport. She just hoped this conference had coffee nearby so she could feel human again.

Charlotte finally made it to the conference center, but she was already ten minutes late from the start of the conference and she still didn't know where she was going. She'd managed to check the start time as she checked into the conference online before she fell asleep in her clothes.

A friendly older lady was waiting by the bank of elevators with a stack of papers.

"Here you go dear; this is a conference booklet to let you know where our sessions will be for the next four days."

"Thank you so much! Do you know if there is coffee anywhere?"

"First floor dear."

"Thank you!" Charlotte called behind her as she grabbed a booklet and jumped onto the elevator. Pouring herself a coffee as she thumbed through the conference booklet to find where she was supposed to be, Charlotte tried to calm her nerves. She found the room she was looking for, knowing that she couldn't miss this one, it was the most important if she wanted to learn the new software for her University!

Charlotte tried to open the door to the session as quietly as she could, but the old door creaked as she pushed it open. Feeling her cheeks glowing, she muttered an apology and snuck to the back of the room, she daren't even look at the presenter, or the sea of eyes boring into her. She wanted the ground to swallow her up, but even as late as she was, she knew she couldn't miss this session, she'd just have to stay behind and apologize to the presenter when the session was over.

When she settled into her seat, and delicately pulled her notepad and pen from her bag, she finally looked up at the presenter, and her heart stopped. It was him! The guy from the coffee shop was standing right there, at the front of the room, staring right at her. Charlotte couldn't breathe. What a small world! How was he here? Maybe if she listened, she'd find out, but all she could hear was the sound of her own breath escaping her lips. Was she staring? She was staring. She needed to calm down. Taking a deep breath, Charlotte told herself to settle down and start paying attention, her promotion depended on it.

....

As Callum started to ease into his conference session, his nerves dissipating as he spoke, he noticed the door opening in the corner of his eye. There's always the stragglers, especially on the first day of any conference, it was to be expected really. He turned his gaze to the figure walking into his session and suddenly he realized he hadn't spoken for a minute, maybe longer, as recognition seized his brain. It was her, the girl who had bumped into him in the coffee house and who had plagued his dreams all night. He wished he'd got her name yesterday, but maybe he could now. Should he call her out for being late? No, no, that was mean. As their gazes locked for a second, he couldn't take his eyes off her until the sight of her pulling her tongue across her lips had his stomach in knots, among other things.

"Concentrate Callum", he told himself firmly as he returned to the group and the session at hand. Software, you're talking about software.

....

As the session got going again, Charlotte finally relaxed and was able to notice the firm, yet gentle, way the presenter had of approaching both the topic and his audience. He was relaxing to listen to and really engaged in the subject, making the whole group pay attention and really learn about the software he was presenting about. Because she had come in late, she'd missed his name, but hoped she would get the chance to find out soon. When she looked down at her lap, she'd written quite a few notes! Normally, when she was listening to training sessions back home, she would have doodled by now, but here she was making pages and pages of detailed notes that she couldn't wait to review later. If she could grasp this material, she would be in a better position to lead the team back home and then the promotion would be hers for sure, trial or no trial!

"Callum, can you go over the last part again please?" someone asked from the audience. Callum. That was his name. While he was busy answering the question, Charlotte took the opportunity to look him over. She had remembered him exactly as he was. He was tall, his hair looked almost black, even in the unflattering lights of the conference center, and he looked strong. Charlotte could tell that beneath his navy-blue polo shirt and dark grey pants, Callum was built like a highland warrior. As she looked over his body, she saw the way his polo sleeves strained against his bulging biceps when he reached to point something out on his presentation. Licking her lips, she crossed her legs to placate the tingle she felt between them and looked up, straight into Callum's deep blue eyes.

....

Callum had tried to ignore the beauty sitting at the back of the room or he knew he would forget what the heck he was supposed to be talking about again. As he paused to give the room a chance to process the section of the presentation he'd been asked to repeat, he looked over at her. She was looking him up and down. The motion of her crossing her legs made her short skirt ride further up her leg, and the sight of her licking her lips had his cock groaning against his pants. Their eyes met and his cock jumped. He needed to pull himself together if he was going to get out of this conference session with his mind, and dignity, intact.

....

As the group began to dissipate, all Charlotte could think about was finding coffee. That first one she had grabbed on the way into the session had gone cold by the time her embarrassment had gone enough for her to dare to pick it up. She needed a caffeine hit, and quickly, but she remembered she needed to apologize to Callum for coming in late and disrupting his session.

She bit back the feeling of needing to run away, smoothed down her skirt, picked up her things and made her way to the front of the room. Callum was chatting to another woman when she reached him. Charlotte took the opportunity to eye up the woman he was talking to. She was thin, beautiful, blonde and caked in make-up. The sort of woman you see at the gym in full make-up, looking like she just stepped out of a magazine instead of having just completed a full work out. Callum looked over at Charlotte and she smiled sweetly, waiting for her turn to talk to him. The other woman was trying to get his attention back, and as he slowly turned his gaze back to her, he wrapped up their conversation. Turning his full attention back to Charlotte, she felt her stomach lurch. Keep it together, girl. She told herself to calm her nerves.

"Hi, I'm Callum". He extended a perfectly large hand for her to take.

"Charlotte. Pleased to meet you." She took his hand and felt electricity sizzle between them. Looking up to meet his blue eyes, she tried to formulate the words and make her mouth say them. She licked her lips to help the words escape.

"I… uh… wanted to apologize… for coming in late. I'd overslept and didn't really know where I was going so… I'm sorry I interrupted your session." She stammered and mentally kicked herself for sounding like a lovestruck teenager.

"Oh, that's ok. The coffee yesterday didn't keep you up did it? It can be mighty strong at that shop." He remembered her. Great, now he thought she was a clutz for bumping into him and had poor time management for being late.

"Uh no, I like it strong. That coffee shop was a perfect start to my stay actually. It's a great place to watch people."

"Yes. I go there often to do just that."

"Well, thank you for your session. It's really interesting to me and pertinent to my job back home. We're implementing this software and I hope to lead the team to do so." She wasn't sure why she was telling him all this, but he was smiling down at her as the words were falling out of her mouth, so she felt encouraged to go on.

"It's actually something I teach at the University, that is, when I'm not teaching them about literature. If you'd like to know more, I'd love to help you get ahead, maybe over coffee?"

Oh my gosh, did he ask just her out? No, no, don't be silly. He wants to help. Besides, after Aiden, Charlotte knew better than to mix business with pleasure, even if this pleasure would be particularly difficult to resist. She bit her lip before she answered.

"I'd love to, actually. Let me give you my cell number and when you're free, I'd like to get coffee."

"Ok. I'll be in touch later today. I'm sure you have a lot of more interesting conference sessions to get to."

"Haha, well obviously this was my favorite one, but you're right, I should get to my next one before I'm late… again."

Charlotte hurried out the door, glancing back to make sure she had all of her things, and made eye contact with Callum one last time. He smiled at her and her insides did a little flip. She bit her lip, smiled back, and went to find her next conference session room. As she discarded her coffee cup, she hoped there was food somewhere along the way, her stomach was not happy that all she'd eaten was a granola bar, but she didn't have any more airport food in her bag.

....

Callum watched as Charlotte left the room, her generous backside swaying hypnotically as she made her way to the exit. He found it hard to think straight when she bit her lip and smiled up at him. The gesture went straight to his pants every time and he wondered how he could get through the next few hours of the conference without thinking about her nonstop. After all, she's all he could think about last night, and now she's here. What a small world. Though, I guess a lot of folks are in town for the same conference, but of all the sessions in all the rooms, she had to walk into his. He found himself growing excited at the thought of their coffee date later. He was going to make it one she wouldn't forget, and he couldn't wait to find out more about the beautiful stranger who'd crossed his path twice now.

....

3.

"Urgh, I'm so tired. These sessions are just never ending!" Diane yawned as she finished her sentence and grabbed her coffee cup.

"I know! This coffee is not strong enough, and my stomach is starting to growl." Charlotte was feeling the strain of jet lag on top of all these conference sessions. She was glad to have made at least one friend in Diane to share her moans with.

"I'm getting kind of hungry too, maybe we should take a look around the conference center and see if we can find anything that looks edible." Diane started to get up before Charlotte could respond.

"Sounds like a great idea", Charlotte mumbled as she hurried to catch up to Diane, who was already starting to walk off.

The conference center was huge, and really colorful from the outside. Inside, there were a lot of floor to ceiling windows, which made you feel like you were in a giant cube at times.

Charlotte watched as Diane looked around each corner to look for something good to eat. Diane looked around the same age as Charlotte's thirty years, she was also much shorter than Charlotte, but made up for it by wearing giant stiletto heels. How she was walking so fast on those tiny points, Charlotte had no idea!

Diane had short red hair, cut into a little bob that fell just below her ears, and smoothed out to make it straight with a little tuck under her chin. She was beautiful, made more so by her gentle Irish accent that seemed to slip into something stronger as she got more tired and hungry.

"Ya know what Charlie, I think we need to go further afield. I don't think there's more than finger sandwiches and stale biscuits here." Diane looked exasperated with those options.

"I saw a little bakery earlier when I went to get some fresh air. It's really close by, shall we go there? I bet they have strong coffee too!" Charlotte started to get excited about the thought of little pastries and hot coffee.

"Oh perfect! I could eat like three of those little cupcakes!" Diane licked her lips and did a little bounce. Charlotte couldn't help but think Diane wouldn't be able to fit more than one little cupcake in her stomach, she was so slender and petite. Unlike Charlotte, who had to workout for a week straight after she'd sniffed the inside of a bakery!

....

As the two located the bakery across the street from the conference center, Charlotte began to get excited at the smell of freshly baked pastries wafting from the open door. To her, there was no better smell than the mix of fresh baking and freshly brewed coffee.

"Oh my!" Diane was looking back and forth along the food case, clearly struggling to decide which item to choose.

"Oh wow! There are so many!" Charlotte was going to have the same problem.

The lady behind the counter chuckled at them as she came over to welcome them into the bakery. Taking the opportunity to look around as Diane started chatting about the selection with the clerk, Charlotte noticed little cafe seats lined up with small tables on one side, and a to-go coffee station on the other side of the bakery. Everything was decorated in pink and yellow, even the clerk's apron matched the decor. Just like the coffee shop she was in yesterday, Charlotte got a relaxing feeling from the bakery, and she couldn't wait to pick something out and get to know her new friend.

"Alright, I'm going with carrot cake! What will you have Charlie? It's on me!" Diane was smiling up at Charlotte.

"Are you sure? That's so kind of you!" Charlotte wasn't used to a stranger being so kind. She took a look at the carrot cake Diane was showing her.

"That looks so good, I'll have the same please, and a cappuccino, thank you Diane." Charlotte felt her stomach starting to audibly growl as the clerk got the carrot cake plated.

Charlotte followed Diane to a table at the back of the bakery.

"I hate sitting in the window, there's nothing worse than people staring at you when you're trying to eat a sticky cake!" Diane said as she sat down.

"Haha, I don't know, usually I'm the one watching the person eating the sticky cake! I love to watch people." Charlotte found it comforting to watch passersby, but she understood not wanting someone to see her shoveling this carrot cake into her mouth.

As they ate, Charlotte and Diane chatted about the conference sessions they'd seen so far, what they had enjoyed and the ones they found really dull. Feeling comfortable, Charlotte took the chance to confide in her new friend about the first session she'd been to, omitting any details of Callum and his presentation skills.

"Ah, I'm glad you made it in! I would have died right there and then if I'd been so late and everyone was staring at me!" Diane was laughing as she finished up her carrot cake.

"Haha, I almost did! I was bright red I'm sure!" Charlotte could feel her cheeks starting to warm as she remembered the morning's embarrassment. Her mind wandered to the moment her and Callum's eyes met during his presentation and she found herself shifting in her seat.

"Right, eat up! We've got to get back to finish the last two sessions! Then we're through the first day!" Diane was already wiping her hands on her napkin and getting ready to leave.

"Are you going to the social thing tonight? You know, the one in the brochure?" Charlotte wanted to go to the First Night Bonanza, but was afraid to go alone, she hoped she could convince her new friend to go with her.

"Aye, I'll go, if you'll go with me and promise not to leave me side?"

"You read my mind! I'll meet you in the hotel lobby at 5?"

"Sounds grand!"

They dropped their trash in the bin on the way out of the bakery, and as Charlotte whirled around to take a step out into the cool Edinburgh air, she bumped straight into Callum.

"You should really start watching where you're going." Callum grinned down at Charlotte. She could see Diane gaping from the corner of her eye.

"I'm so sorry! I don't know why I keep bumping into you! I swear I don't make a habit of running down strange men."

"Ah so you think I'm strange, huh?"

"No, no, I just meant…."

"I know what you meant, you're fine." Callum's smile reached his eyes as he playfully teased her for her lack of situational awareness.

"Enjoying the conference so far?" He asked.

"Yes, just two more sessions left before the First Night Bonanza." Charlotte realized that as a conference presenter, Callum would most likely be attending too. She found herself hoping he would be.

"Ah yeah. They do that every year. It's good, you should go."

"Are… I mean, will you be going?"

"No, not this time, I have to prepare to teach my class at the University in the morning." Callum's expression changed. Charlotte wondered if he'd sensed her disappointment at his answer.

"I haven't forgotten our date, though." He smiled at her again.

"Our… date?" Charlotte must have looked confused because Callum outright laughed. It was such a warm sound; it made her smile.

"Our coffee date… to talk about my software…", he was still smiling at her.

"Oh right, yes. Just message me when you have time to go. I only have morning sessions at the conference tomorrow."

"Well that's great, I'm only teaching one class tomorrow. Maybe I can pick you up from the conference at lunch?"

"Ok, see you then!" Charlotte couldn't hide the grin that had started to spread across her face. She mentally kicked herself for getting excited over their coffee date. No business with pleasure, remember! She scolded herself internally and reminded herself that this was just a coffee, with a very hot Scotsman, to learn about software that would save her promotion.

"So...", the sound of Diane's expectant voice pulled Charlotte from her thoughts.

"Hmm?" was all she could muster.

"The hot guy with the hot accent... what's that about?" Diane was very straightforward, it was refreshing.

"Ah, no, I just keep bumping into him is all, literally actually. He's going to help me with that software issue I was telling you about." Charlotte tried her best to sound disinterested in the hot stranger, but she couldn't deny that he was quite the specimen of a man.

"Ok ok, well he's totally into you."

"What?! No, no, it's not like that I swear!"

"Haha, well let's get back to the conference then. I can't wait to hear all about your hot Scotsman during the Bonanza. Now that's a place to people watch!"

Despite the heat rising in her cheeks, Charlotte was actually looking forward to letting loose a little at the Bonanza. She'd never been to anything like that, and it would be a welcome escape from the realities of her own situation. She made the decision there and then to let tonight be a chance to really let her hair down and enjoy being far away from her problems.

....

4.

"Finally,", Charlotte muttered to herself after the final conference session of the day had finished. She stuffed her notebook into her bag and silently reflected on the day. She'd learned a good deal about her industry and different types of software that her University might be able to use in the future, but she was keen to know more about the software she'd need to become an expert in so she could lead her team and win that promotion for good.

Stepping outside into the cool air, Charlotte began walking toward the rank of taxi cabs waiting across the street from the conference center. Luckily there were a few waiting, so she grabbed the first one and slid into the backseat. She checked her watch to see how much time she had to get to the hotel and get ready for the First Night Bonanza. Ok, two hours to get ready and grab a light snack, plenty of time!

As the taxicab whirred through the city, and wound itself expertly through the narrow roads, Charlotte settled into the ride. She was feeling proud of herself for coming all this way and taking a chance on her future. She thought for sure that if she could just learn enough to show her worth back home, then there was no way the University and the Dean could deny her the promotion, that is, unless Aiden stopped them somehow. She shook her head to clear the image of him and the bad feeling it always brought to the pit of her stomach. No, she wouldn't think of him on this trip, he wouldn't ruin this for her too.

"We're here lass", the sound of the taxi driver's thick Scottish accent pulled her from her thoughts.

"Oh, thank you!" Paying him, she stepped out of the taxi and hurried up to her hotel room. She was thankful that her new friend, Diane, was at the same hotel.

As soon as the keycard unlocked her room, she threw down her bag and peeled off her conference clothes. She turned on the shower and waited for it to heat up before she stepped into the warming stream of water. Sighing as she felt the weight of her problems ease into the water stream, Charlotte finally started to feel serene in her new surroundings.

Turning off the shower with a squeak, she grabbed a big fluffy towel from under the sink. Wrapping the towel around herself, she padded into the bedroom and thumbed through her clothes. "Aha!" Charlotte forgot that she had packed a few cute dresses, just in case there were any social activities that she would need to prepare for.

Sometime later, Charlotte was standing in front of the bathroom mirror, ready to go down to meet Diane for the Bonanza. She had lightly curled her hair and put on fresh make up for the occasion. The dress she wore was deep green with short capped sleeves and hugged her curves all the way to her knee. She paired the dress with some block heel sandals and gave herself one final look before heading out.

....

"Wow! Look at you!" Diane was waiting by the reception desk when Charlotte stepped off the elevator.

"Haha, oh hush, look at you!" Charlotte laughed off the compliment, Diane was much prettier than her and had gone with a short grey skirt and matching peplum top for the occasion, with the same dangerously high stilettos she'd been wearing earlier.

"Seriously, you look amazing!" Diane was smiling at Charlotte, but she was secretly pleased that she thought she looked good. Charlotte couldn't deny that she was hoping Callum would change his mind and come to the Bonanza, even though he said he'd have too much work to do.

"So, I heard that the conference was going to lay on buses for us and pick people up from the surrounding hotels. We just have to wait outside." Diane always seemed to know what was happening, she always had up-to-date information.

"Ok great, let's step outside and wait".

Just as they stepped outside, a big coach came around the corner with the conference logo across the side. They stepped closer to the edge of the hotel entrance and waited for it to stop.

Climbing up the stairs to the coach, Charlotte stopped in her tracks and Diane almost bumped into the back of her. Callum? She could have sworn he was sitting at the back of the bus, but it was too dark to really know for sure. Sensing the annoyance of the bus driver, she found the closest empty seats and sat down, motioning for Diane to sit next to her.

"Did you see? Is that Callum at the back of the bus?" she asked Diane.

"Who's Callum?" Oh right, Charlotte had forgotten she was too tongue tied to actually introduce the two earlier.

"Oh, right, right, the guy outside of the bakery earlier. Tall, really dark hair, gorgeous blue eyes…", she'd started to waffle.

"Ah you mean the guy you have a thing for but won't admit? I didn't see, shall I go and check?" Diane had a playful tone to her voice, but Charlotte believed she would absolutely go and check in the most unsubtle way.

"No, please don't. He said he was working so I must be seeing things." Charlotte laughed lightly and stared out of the window.

Sitting back into the coach seat, Charlotte looked out of the window for most of the ride to the Bonanza. Seeing the city as dusk fell was more beautiful than she could ever have imagined. Edinburgh was starting to become the most beautiful place she'd ever visited, and she tried to push back thoughts of having to leave in a few weeks. Once again, she silently praised herself for extending her trip beyond the conference.

"Alright lads and lasses, here we are then." The bus driver opened the doors and waited for everyone to get off.

Diane jumped up and got into the line to exit the bus. Charlotte grabbed her bag and lined up behind three other people.

"Hi there." Charlotte recognized the silky-smooth voice echoing in her ear. The sensation of breath on the nape of her neck had head pooling in her stomach. Turning around slowly to confirm the face behind the familiar voice, she found herself slowly smiling up at Callum.

"I thought you had work to do." she breathed.

"Ah well, I finished early and couldn't resist a bonanza, and the chance to see you again." He smiled down at her, a smile that reached his eyes, and she felt all warm and tingly.

Stepping off the bus, Charlotte spotted Diane motioning her over. This time she remembered to introduce her two new friends, much to the delight of Diane who was grinning from ear to ear.

"Pleasure to meet you Callum, won't you join us for drinks?" She cooed.

"I'd love to, sure." Callum answered Diane, but he was looking right at Charlotte.

Charlotte and Callum followed behind Diane and she led them into the Bonanza. The conference organizers had rented out an old museum to function as their Bonanza venue. Food tables filled with hors d'oeuvres lined the edges of a large area, in the center of which was a small band and dance floor. At the back of the room, Charlotte could see a large bar, she must've seen it at the same time as Diane because the latter made a beeline straight for it.

"What'll it be, lass? Wine? Beer?" Callum's deep voice burned her earlobes.

"Actually, I'm more of a scotch person", a slow smile spread across Charlotte's face as she registered slight shock on Callum's face.

"A woman after my own heart! Two glasses of scotch please, neat." Callum turned his attention to the bar attendant, then handed me a glass.

Taking a sip, the warm liquid burned her throat as it made its way down into her gullet. Swallowing, she looked up at Callum, then decided to take a second sip to calm the nerves that were threatening to envelop her.

"I'm going to go dance, catch you later." Diane's Irish drawl drew her attention away from Callum.

"Have fun! I might join you later!" I yelled after her as she gave me a wave.

"Come with me", Charlotte's attention snapped back to Callum as he held out his hand for her. As she took it, a jolt of electricity shot up her arm and excitement pooled in her belly. Licking her lips, she followed him to the bottom of a spiral staircase at the front of the museum. His grasp on her hand hardened as he wound his fingers around hers and led her up the staircase to a balcony overlooking the dance floor.

The room was dark, with multicolored spotlights shining down onto the dance floor. The only lights coming from next to the food tables at the sides of the room. Charlotte could smell the cologne coming from Callum, it was a rich, earthy scent that drew her in and made her think of old camping trips with her father. It was safe, but on Callum, it was sexy. Music from the band below filled her ears. Her senses overwhelmed by the music and the scent of Callum's cologne made her feel dizzy. She looked over at Callum and saw he was gazing at her intently from behind his scotch glass.

She smiled up at him and he smiled back, still gently holding her hand with fingers entwined.

"Do you want to dance?" he raised an eyebrow as he asked.

"I quite like being here on the balcony", she wasn't ready to go back and rejoin the party just yet.

"Who says we have to rejoin the others, we don't need a dance floor when we have music", as if he read her mind, he propped his glass on the ledge of the balcony and moved behind her.

With one hand still entwined with hers, he used the other to hold onto the balcony, his front to her back, she was enclosed in his arms. Charlotte felt her hips start to move to the music as she gently danced in front of Callum. She could feel him gently against her behind.

"I'm glad you decided to come", she whispered, not sure if he would even be able to hear her.

"I'm glad too", he whispered into her ear.

As the music continued to play, Charlotte felt the beat inside her and allowed her body to move along to the rhythm, not caring that Callum could probably feel every hip movement. She tipped her head back, making eye contact with Callum. She bit her lip and continued to sway with her head almost resting on Callum's shoulder.

"Bite your lip at me again and I might just have to bite it for you", he growled into her ear.

Whether the scotch had taken effect, or she was simply overtaken by Callum's presence, she wasn't sure, but she wanted to feel him, she wanted to feel what it would be like for him to nibble on her lip. Encouraged by her surroundings and the scotch, she gave a wicked smile to Callum, then bit her lip again.

The sound of Callum groaning, and the sensation of him gently pulling on her lip with his teeth had heat pooling between Charlotte's legs. She groaned as Callum's lips met hers. As he deepened the kiss, his hands went to her hips and pulled her around to face him. Charlotte pressed her body as tightly as she could to Callum's, wanting desperately to be closer to him. Groaning at the feel of her body against his, Callum clung tighter to her hips, making them buck under his touch. She moved her hands under his jacket to dig her nails lightly into his back, clinging onto him as she felt his tongue lap against hers. The sensation increasing her urgency to have him closer to her, wanting him to take her there and then on the balcony, not caring who could see them.

....

5.

"Ladies and gentlemen, the buffet tables are now open!" The booming sound of the microphone broke the spell between Charlotte and Callum.

Stepping back from his grasp, Charlotte gasped and touched her hand to her lips.

"I'm sorry", she stammered.

"Sorry? You have nothing to be sorry for." Callum was just as breathless as she was.

"We should... um", Charlotte wasn't quite sure what she wanted to say, but gestured vaguely toward the downstairs area.

"Uh, yes, let's get some food", Callum seemed confused.

Making their way down to the food tables, the two fell into an awkward silence. Charlotte wasn't sure what had happened, but the air between them seemed to change. She had enjoyed the kiss, her lips still felt the tingle of his caress, but she had promised herself not to get involved with someone in a professional setting again. Then again, she didn't work with Callum, it wasn't the same situation that she'd had with Aiden. Maybe she could let herself enjoy Callum, at least while she was away from home, but from the look on his face, she wasn't sure if she had already blown it.

....

"What just happened?" Callum thought to himself as he approached the food tables. He wasn't normally one for so obvious public displays of affection, especially with women he'd only just met. There was just something about Charlotte that he couldn't shake off. He didn't really know her and yet he couldn't stop thinking about her, and that kiss… That is something he wouldn't forget for a while. He wondered what had made her apologize. He felt terrible, like he'd been punched in the gut when she'd apologized to him. Maybe he should give her some space, not that he wanted to.

....

Piling up her plate, Charlotte couldn't resist all of the delicious looking finger food at the food tables. Callum had left her to talk to a colleague of his, so she looked around for Diane. Spotting her leaning on the bar, Charlotte headed over.

"Hey, how's it going?" Charlotte mumbled through a mouthful of food.

"Ya know, that food looks so much better when it's half hanging out of your mouth", Diane laughed through her sarcastic comment.

"Sorry, I'm stress eating."

"Why are you stressed?" Diane looked questioningly at Charlotte.

"Um, no reason, really." There was no way she was going to tell Diane what just happened with Callum.

"Hey, isn't that your guy?" Charlotte dropped her mouthful of food as she slowly turned in the direction Diane was pointing. Just then, Callum spotted her and seemed to make a beeline toward them.

"Hey, care to dance?" He smiled down at Charlotte and she almost dropped her plate.

"Uh… sure."

"Here, I'll take that…" Diane took Charlotte's plate from her and gently pushed her into Callum's arms. As they danced, Charlotte looked up into Callum's deep blue eyes and couldn't help but smile. When she was with him, she didn't feel as self-conscious as she did when she was thinking about him, or rather, overthinking.

"You're so beautiful", he purred into her ear and she felt her insides melt. Maybe a holiday romance is just what she needed, she thought, as she let herself move to the music against his strong body.

Charlotte couldn't help but get closer to Callum, and as the music slowed to a soft song, he pulled her in closer still. Their bodies were tightly touching, while her arms creeped up his body to circle his neck, his gently caressing her hips until they stopped short of cupping her backside. They swayed together like that for some time until she looked up at him and they locked eyes. He smiled as he bent down to kiss her. This time, the kiss was gentle and exploring, she kissed him back softly.

"Let's get out of here", she whispered. She knew it was risky, but she had already decided to let this happen, and she couldn't resist Callum anymore.

Before she had a chance to change her mind, Callum was already grabbing her hand and heading to the exit. He hoped the coach was ready to go.

Climbing up the stairs of the coach, there was no-one on board as the two made their way to the back and slid into the seats, still holding hands. Callum couldn't wait until they were back in the hotel, he had to have her now.

Moving toward her, he cupped the side of her face and kissed her, as she leaned into his hand and kissed him back with urgency. He could feel his cock harden against his pants, but he didn't care, he wanted her to feel him. As if she read his mind, her hand slowly made its way to his thigh, grazing her nails into his pants as she pushed her hand further toward his groin, and his throbbing member.

Charlotte gasped as she felt the length of his penis through his pants. She smiled hungrily as she began kissing him again and moving her hand to feel him grow under her touch.

Callum groaned as he deepened the kiss. His hand moving from the back of Charlotte's neck to the top of her knee. His hand slid gently until he found her center. She gasped as she bucked her hips closer to him, demanding to be touched. As his fingers started to explore her, the sound of the bus door opening had them both jumping back into their seats.

Flustered, Charlotte sat bolt upright in her seat, frightened someone would have seen them. What was she thinking?! She needed to get a grip on herself and get to the hotel as fast as she could. Sneaking a glimpse at Callum, she had the feeling he felt the same way.

....

As the bus got to her hotel, she stood up and almost pulled Callum with her. They hurried to the front of the bus and jumped off as fast as they could. Thanking the bus driver, Charlotte had already started to fumble in her bag for her key before they'd even approached the hotel entrance. They marched toward the elevator bank and she punched in the button to go up. Callum's hands were wrapped around her waist as they stepped onto the elevator and she punched the button for her floor. Luckily the elevator was empty, as Callum pulled her in for a kiss.

"If you don't quit, we won't make it to the hotel room', she purred.

He grinned as she bit her lip and kissed him one last time before the elevator reached her floor. Sliding the key into the door lock, she swung open her hotel room door and Callum hurriedly followed behind her. Shutting the door, she turned around as Callum trapped her with his arm against the door by her head. She smiled as he leant down to kiss her. His urgent kiss deepened until she moaned against his breath.

She reached for his shirt and began unbuttoning them. Yanking his shirt tails free, she grazed her hands up into his thick chest hair, loving the feel of the soft hair beneath her fingers. He pulled her closer, still kissing her deeply, and slowly unzipped the back of her dress. Breaking the kiss, he stepped back to allow the hard fabric of her dress to drop to the floor, exposing the soft lines of her body, dressed in matching black lace bra and panties.

"Wow, you're just so… wow", he almost growled at her as he reached for her again.

She grabbed his belt buckle and started to undo it, kissing him as she worked his belt free. Callum gently moved her hands back so he could free himself from his pants and underwear. Charlotte gasped and dropped to her knees as his long, thick and hard penis sprang free. She looked up at him and smiled, licking her lips, before she took his length into her mouth. He growled as sensations rocked through him and he struggled to hold onto the edge. He couldn't hold it much longer, the feel of her hot, wet mouth on his dick was making him crazy, he needed her. Pulling her to her feet, he laid her gently on the bed.

Despite not yet being touched where she needed it, Charlotte felt close to the edge already. She couldn't wait much longer, she needed to feel him inside her. As she tried to find the words to tell him, he was by her side. He lowered the straps of her bra, limiting her arm movements, and freed one of her soft mounds. Taking her nipple into his mouth, he gently nibbled until a moan escaped Charlotte's lips. Freeing her other breast, he repeated his pleasure until Charlotte couldn't take any more. She reached for his manhood and pleaded with her eyes for him to take her.

"Please… I need…", she rasped out, her chest heaving with desire.

Callum wound his fingers underneath her panties and felt her soft, warm center.

"You're so ready for me", his greedy eyes hungered for her. In one swift move, he removed her panties and slid into her, bringing her to climax with every stroke.

"Oh Callum…." Charlotte rode out her climax, but Callum wasn't done. He continued to thrust deep inside her until he couldn't take any more, he needed release. They came together one final time before Callum collapsed on the bed next to her.

Gently scooping her into his arms, they lay together sated and sweaty, waiting for their breathing to go from rough to calm.

As Callum held her in his arms, Charlotte started to feel something deep within her heart, a feeling she hadn't felt for a very long time. A feeling she didn't want to acknowledge.

"Callum?" she started to ask if he felt something, but luckily thought better of it. He didn't answer, he was already gently snoring.

....

Charlotte woke with a start. She wasn't sure where she was. She'd been dreaming about Aiden and must have woken herself up. It was pitch black in the room. She could hear soft snoring in the darkness, Callum. A smile came to her lips as heat filled her and she remembered what they'd done a few hours before. Carefully peeling back the sheet that covered her, Charlotte crept into the bathroom to freshen up and brush her teeth.

As she climbed back into bed, Callum stirred.

"Charlotte…?"

"It's ok, I just had a bad dream. Go back to sleep."

"Mmmhmm…"

Charlotte settled into the bedsheets. Callum pulled her closer toward his body. She could feel his growing erection against the small of her back. Positioning herself so that she could feel him against her butt cheeks, she gently moved her hips to entice him.

"Mmm", he moaned under her swaying movements.

Callum brought his hand from around her waist to cup her breast. He gently pinched her nipple, which made Charlotte fling her head back and expose her neck. As Callum continued his assault on her nipple, he began kissing her neck. Charlotte adjusted her body to give Callum better access to where she really wanted him to be. Sensing what she needed, he entered her from behind in one long stroke.

"Callum…", gasping his name, Charlotte rocked back and forth, savoring the feel of him inside her. His penis felt like it had been carved from marble and made especially for her.

Coming together, Callum withdrew himself and pulled Charlotte against his body. Flopping a proprietary arm around her waist, they fell into a sound sleep together.

□.□.□.□.

6.

*beep**beep**beep**

Once again, the sound of the alarm awoke Charlotte from the deepest sleep, she'd ever been in. This time, as she opened her eyes and slammed her hand on the button to shut off the alarm, she felt the warmth of Callum behind her.

"Mmm, good morning beautiful", that Scottish drawl was even more sexy first thing in the morning.

"Good morning, handsome."

Callum watched as Charlotte made her way to the bathroom. She was completely naked but didn't seem to mind a bit that he was lazily staring at her as she padded across the room. He loved a woman with confidence. After last night, Callum had full faith that her confidence was earned, she knew her way around the bedroom!

Charlotte looked into the mirror and grunted; her hair looked like she'd been dragged through a hedge backward. Turning on the shower, she tried to tame her hair as the water heated up. As she stepped into the warm water, Callum came in behind her, kissing her neck.

"Callum… I have to get to the conference. There isn't time for round… um", Charlotte couldn't even remember how many times they'd been intimate last night.

"Mmm ok, I suppose I can wait. Are you feeling ok? Sore?"

"A little, but in the best way!" Charlotte felt like she'd slept for years, her body ached from the night before.

Callum stepped out of the shower, grabbing a towel and wrapping it around his waist. His muscles bulged as he reached for a second towel. Wrapping the towel around Charlotte, Callum lifted her out of the shower and laid a kiss on the top of her forehead. She smiled, then sidestepped him to finish getting ready. She didn't want to be late and Callum was such a distraction.

"Do you have time for breakfast?" Callum was already dressed in last night's clothes, waiting for her to come out of the bathroom.

"Uh, not really no", Charlotte checked her watch and really wished she had more time in the mornings.

"How about lunch?" He seemed hopeful.

"Absolutely! I'm starving! Can we talk about the software over something hearty?" She wanted to make sure she at least had the chance to talk over the software he created before she was distracted by him again.

"Oh yeah, that would be great! I'll meet you outside of the conference center at noon."

"Ok, I'll be there."

"I'm counting on it. Want me to take a cab to the conference with you?"

"No, it's ok. I think Diane is coming with me, she's in this hotel too."

"Ok, I'll see you later." Callum bent down to kiss her on the forehead, then left her alone in the hotel room.

Sighing, Charlotte sat on the bed to get her things together and put her shoes on. She pulled her phone from her bag and texted Diane.

ARE YOU UP?
YES. READY?

I'M READY. MEET YOU IN THE LOBBY IN 5.

....

Charlotte and Diane barely spoke in the taxicab on the way to the conference. Charlotte was aching and thinking about the night before, while Diane looked worse for wear, probably also thinking about the night before.

As the two walked into the conference center, a large table had been set up at the entrance. It was filled with pastries, mini muffins and coffee. Oh, thank Jesus, Charlotte thought to herself. Coffee and carbs were exactly what her body needed. Clearly Diane was thinking the same thing as she made a beeline to the table.

Taking their food and coffee to go, they headed to the first conference session.

"Which one are you going to?" Charlotte turned to speak to Diane before shoving a pastry into her mouth.

"Girl, I don't even know my own name yet. I drank way too much last night. I'm going wherever you're going, ya know, in case I need a crutch."

Laughing gently, Charlotte guided her friend to the first conference session, and they found seats at the back, close to the door in case they needed to leave. This was going to be a long morning, but Charlotte was excited for her lunch date.

....

As noon rolled around, Charlotte found her way to the entrance of the conference center. Diane had long gone, having ducked out around 10am, just before the end of the second session.

"Hey, you ready to eat?" Callum approached her looking as tired as she felt.

"Didn't get much sleep last night, huh?" Charlotte couldn't help but tease the handsome man who stood before her.

"Funnily enough, I had better things to do than sleep last night", his wink brought her to her knees.

"Let's eat!" Charlotte licked her lips at the suggestion. She took his proffered arm as he led the way to lunch.

"Where are we going?" They'd rounded the corner and walked further than Charlotte had ventured before. Her stomach was starting to grumble, and her body still ached from the night before.

"You'll see", Callum grinned down at her.

Finally, they stopped and Callum held the door open to a large cafe that seemed to double as a bookstore.

"Wow, how beautiful", Charlotte couldn't help but gaze around the cafe. Bookshelves covered every wall from floor to ceiling, while cafe tables were placed around the middle of the cafe. Charlotte could smell so many delicious scents, from hot food to coffee and pastries filled the air, making her stomach growl audibly.

"Table for two is it?" A hostess appeared, looking Callum up and down as she spoke.

"Yes please, near a window if possible." Callum seemed oblivious to the attention the hostess was trying to give. She shrugged and led us to a table in the corner with a view of the street outside.

"What a beautiful place."

"I thought you might like it. It's one of my favorite places to come and people watch."

"I love to do that, it's so relaxing."

"It really is. Though, I'd rather watch you."

Charlotte blushed and wasn't sure how to reply. At that point, the waiter came over to take their order. There were so many delicious looking options, she wasn't sure what to choose. Taking Callum's lead, she went with a club sandwich and side of fries with water. She needed to rehydrate from the lack of sleep the night before.

As they ate, they looked out of the window in a comfortable silence, casually watching the world go by. Charlotte couldn't remember the last time she felt so serene.

Breaking into her thoughts was the reminder that she needed to start focusing if she wanted to get that promotion.

"So, you wanted to ask more about the software?" It was as if Callum could read her mind sometimes!

"Yes, see back home I'm trying to get this promotion, but right now I'm under a sort of trial period. They won't let me have the promotion fully unless I can successfully lead a team to implement the software you created."

"Ah, I see. So, you need to get a head start on learning how it works."

"Exactly. Plus, I don't think my superiors really want me to get the promotion, so I need to make sure I do well enough to not give them a reason to overlook me."

"Why would you think that?"

"Well, I kind of have someone back home who isn't exactly in my corner and isn't shy about making that known to the higher-ups."

"That sucks, I'm sorry. Well, the good news is, I created the software and we have two days left of the conference for me to show you everything I know." Callum looked sad as he realized they only had two days left.

"Actually, I extended my stay for two weeks past the conference. I wanted to make the most out of my time in Scotland, and spend some time exploring too." Charlotte smiled over at Callum, his face visibly lit up as she divulged this piece of information.

"That's great news! I have some vacation time from work, I would love to show you around. Edinburgh has always been my home, but there are so many things to see outside of the city too."

"I would love that! As long as you also tell me about the software."

"Absolutely, we'll just do it with a view."

While the two finished their lunch, they talked about the basics of the software and what Charlotte's team was going to use it for. By the time they were finished, Charlotte felt much more positive about what she'd learned and how she could use the information to lead her team. She couldn't wait to explore Scotland with this handsome, talented and educated man.

Callum walked Charlotte back to the conference center after lunch. She had some time before she needed to be back in the sessions.
"Thank you for lunch, I had the best time."

"Better than last night, huh?" Charlotte blushed as Callum reminded her of the night before.

"So, two more days of the conference, right?" He asked.

"Yes, today and tomorrow."

"I have to teach this afternoon, and all-day tomorrow. What's say I finish up work and you finish up the conference, then we can start our tour?"

"Sounds perfect." Charlotte leaned up to kiss Callum on the cheek. Turning at the last minute, Callum gave Charlotte a goodbye kiss that made her toes curl in her boots.

"I can't wait. Have an amazing conference Charlotte, I'll be waiting on the other side."

....

7.

Charlotte went back inside the conference center, excited about what she had to look forward to, her anxiety about the future and her promotion all but gone.

Turning to look for coffee to get her through her next session, Charlotte spotted Diane sitting on a step.

"Are you ok? I thought you went back to the hotel."

"Oh, I did. I napped, stuffed my face with food from the hotel and came back. There's a session this afternoon that I really didn't want to miss, come with me?"

"Sure! There wasn't a specific session I wanted to see over another one this afternoon, I'd love company!"

·········

"I don't know about you, but I'm exhausted." Diane slumped down in the oversized lounge chair opposite Charlotte. The conference center had comfy seating in little nooks and crannies all over the building, supposedly to give conference goers a chance to sit and recharge their electronics.

"Me too. I'm sad the conference ends in two days though!" Charlotte was going to miss this place. It wasn't the first time she was thankful to have extended her stay.

"One really. We're almost done with today."

"That's true. Ugh. It's been such a good few days."

"So, where are we eating tonight? Or, are you planning to meet with your beau?"

"My beau?!"

"I saw you two last night, leaving together on the bus!"

"Oh, that. Well, I wouldn't call him my beau… maybe a vacation romance…?"

"Oooh girl, I wouldn't mind being romanced by a guy that looks like that!"

"Haha, there's still time! Why don't we go out tonight and have dinner and drinks?" I didn't normally go out for drinks back home, but I wanted to make the most of my time with Diane.

"I'm in. Don't let me drink too much though, I still have a headache from last night!"

"Meet you in the hotel lobby at 6?"

"Sounds good to me!"

....

As Charlotte made her way out of the last session of the day, she couldn't wait to have a girl's night with Diane. She had a great time with Callum but having a night to herself without having to overthink was really something special to Charlotte. She had friends back in Seattle, but rarely got the time to go out and just relax, especially when Aiden was around.

Stepping out of the conference center, Charlotte noticed the air had turned and had a chill to it. She pulled her jacket closer together and made her way to the taxi rank. For the first time since she'd been in the city, there were no taxi cab's waiting at the rank, she hoped one would come along soon. Although Charlotte was excited for the night to come, she was also really tired from the night before with Callum. If she got back to the hotel soon, she would have time for a little cat nap before she had to start getting ready. She couldn't wait to sink into the soft, warm hotel sheets.

The wind whipped along and stung Charlotte's eyes and cheeks as she waited for a taxi to appear. She started to pull her phone out of her bag to see about calling for a private hire taxicab when it buzzed in her hand. A text. Charlotte's heart stopped and the chill she felt in her face reached her stomach. Aiden. Throwing her phone back in her bag, she stood shivering, and it wasn't just because of the cold Scottish air.

"Miss…?" The sound of the taxi driver pulled her back to reality.

"Miss, do you need a taxi?" He tried again.

"Oh yes, sorry." Charlotte climbed into the back of the taxi, feeling numb as she parroted off the name of the hotel.

As she slouched into the back of the seat, she slowly pulled out her phone and opened the text.

WHERE ARE YOU?

Not knowing whether or not to reply, Charlotte just stared at the text for a minute. Deciding it was better for her job if she didn't ignore him, she punched out a quick reply and pressed send.

AT CONFERENCE, THEN VACATION.

Three little black dots popped up on the screen. He was replying. Suddenly, the dots disappeared, he'd left her on read. Charlotte released a deep breath she hadn't realized she was holding and got out of the taxicab. She didn't want to deal with Aiden right now.

Charlotte swiped her key card into her hotel room. Deciding to forego a shower, she flopped her bag next to the door and slumped down on the bed. Setting the alarm on her phone to wake her in two hours, she drifted off into a deep sleep.

....

The shrill sound of the phone alarm woke Charlotte with a start. Bolting upright into the bed, she flustered to turn off the alarm. Remembering her earlier text from Aiden, she checked her messages to see if he had replied. One new message. Flicking open her inbox, she was relieved to see Diane's name pop up on the screen.

SEE YOU AT 6. DON'T FORGET. I'M STARVING ALREADY.

Punching out a quick reply, Charlotte plugged her phone into the nightstand to charge and padded to the bathroom. She took her time to redo her make-up, opting for a muted palette for her girl's night.

Padding back into the bedroom, she flicked her suitcase open and thumbed through her options. Sitting cross-legged next to her open case, she finally settled on a fitted deep red dress, knee high tan boots and a denim jacket. It had been chilly when she came to the hotel, so she imagined it would only get more brisk as the night went on. Slipping into her new outfit, she finished the look with a simple red plaid scarf, grabbed her bag and rushed out the door.

"Oh awesome, you're early too." Diane looked amazing in her little black dress and another pair of stilettos.

"You know it's probably freezing out there, right?" Charlotte hated to be too cold, she didn't want her friend getting frozen before they'd even eaten.

"I have a jacket in my bag, we're good to go." Diane turned around to expose a giant tote bag.

"Don't forget the kitchen sink!" Charlotte laughed.

"Haha, hey, it fits everything I need in it! Let's go!"

The two stepped into a waiting taxicab and directed the driver to drop them off in the city center.

Sliding out of the taxicab, Charlotte looked around the city. She'd been right, it was getting colder. Pulling her scarf closer to her chin, and her jacket closer together, she smiled as she looked around. The city was bustling with people waiting to eat, drink and be merry. The air carried people's conversations, and the smells of different cuisines busting out of kitchen and restaurant windows. Her stomach growled audibly.

"Girl, me too. What type of food do you want?" Diane looked just as eager to find food.

"Anything really. There's a pub over there, the smells coming from the doorway are making my mouth water."

"Sounds good to me, let's go."

Pushing the door to the pub open, the two were hit with the stale smell of ale and the warmth from the fireplace hitting their faces.

"Just two?" the hostess appeared, smiling at them as she saw their reaction to the quaint location.

"Yes please. Can we sit near the fireplace?"

"Sure, follow me", the hostess bounced away as they followed. The fireplace was in a small seating area with only about four tables. The bar stretched out from the side of the fireplace to the rest of the bar, where more tables and seating areas rested.

Taking the table closest to the fireplace, the two looked through their menus.

"Can I get you something to drink?' the waitress popped up almost instantaneously.

"I'll take a whiskey please, on the rocks."

"Dry white wine for me please. Charlotte how do you drink whiskey? It's so… sharp."

"Oh, I've always liked it. I had a partner back in Seattle who got me hooked, and now I can't resist. Plus, we're in Scotland, can't leave here without having tried the original."

"Good point!"

Their drinks arrived and they settled into gentle silence as they sipped away, looking at the fireplace. The pub was so quaint and relaxing that Charlotte felt like she could fall asleep at the table. Looking at the menu again, Charlotte decided to try a toad in the hole with fries. It sounded wonderful, though she'd never had it before, she knew it was sausages in a delicious pastry. She wanted some hearty food to keep the night's chill out of her bones. Diane must have felt the same way as she ordered a French onion soup with baguette.

Both meals arrived and the two didn't waste any time tucking in.

"OMG this is delicious". Diane slurped her soup a little as she moaned and gurgled over her bowl.

"This is too. Everything smells so good."

As the two finished off their meal, they looked around the pub.

"Do you want another drink here, or shall we try somewhere else?" Diane thought the pub was a little empty and she really wanted a chance to talk to some locals.

"Let's go somewhere busier and work on that romance of yours."

"Haha, sold! Let's go."

Charlotte tightened her jacket to her once again as they stepped into the street. A group of thirty-somethings were heading to a bar across the way.

"They seem to know where they're going, let's go there." Diane must have seen them too.

The two opened the door into the new pub and found it much busier, and louder. Live music played at the back of the pub. The atmosphere was fluttering with excitement as drinks flowed from the bar taps.

"Now this is more like it!" Diane danced her way to the bar as Charlotte followed, feeling invigorated from the live music and joyous atmosphere.

The two grabbed drinks from the bar and settled at a high-top table, close to the music, but far enough away that they didn't have to shout to hear each other. Just then, two handsome men came over to talk to them.

"Hi, I'm John."

"I'm Taylor. What are two fine ladies like you doing in a place like this?"

"Ah we're just visiting for a conference. It's our last full night." Diane fluttered her eyelashes at the men.

As Diane flirted with the men, Charlotte found herself missing Callum. Maybe she should text him. Reaching into her bag, she was shocked to find her phone was missing. Grasping around, she started to pull items from her purse to see where the phone could be.

"Ah damnit."

"What is it?" Diane looked concerned.

"I left my phone at the hotel." Remembering she'd put it on the nightstand to charge, Charlotte kicked herself for not taking the time to pick it up before she left.

"Do you need to use mine?" Diane offered her phone, but Charlotte didn't know Callum's number off by heart.

"Uh no, you're fine. Thanks though."

....

After dancing, drinking and watching Diane flirt for what seemed like hours, Charlotte was ready to fall into her hotel bed.

"Hey, are you ready to head back to the hotel soon?" She had to shout over the music to get Diane's attention.

"Actually yes, my feet are killing me!"

Diane excused herself from the two handsome men and the pair left the bar. It was almost freezing outside, though the alcohol the two had consumed probably helped them at least get to the taxi rank. Jumping into the first taxicab, they headed off to the hotel.

When they got to the hotel, they said their goodnight's in the lobby and headed to their separate rooms. Charlotte was exhausted and couldn't wait to fall asleep. Tomorrow was the last day of the conference and Charlotte didn't want to miss any of the sessions.

She was also hoping to get hold of Callum to have another conversation about the new software she was wanting to implement back home. After their conversation the day before, she was keen to follow up with him, though if she were being honest with herself, it wasn't entirely because of the software.

Charlotte got herself ready for bed and slipped under the covers. She pulled her phone from the nightstand and saw a missed call and two new messages. Opening up the messages first, she froze.

I'M COMING TO GET YOU. YOU SHOULD BE HOME, WITH ME.

It was from Aiden. The missed call was from him too. She didn't reply. She didn't have anything to say to him and she sure as hell didn't want to think about him right now, especially before bed. He wouldn't know exactly where she was anyway, and besides, Callum was taking her away to see the countryside once the conference ended. He'd never find her then.

The second message was from Aiden.

I MISS YOU. DINNER TOMORROW?

She wondered if it was too late to reply, but she didn't care. She typed out a message and hit send before falling asleep with the phone in her hand.

I MISS YOU TOO. MEET ME AT 7 BY THE CONFERENCE CENTER?

....

8.

Charlotte woke up from a restless night's sleep. All night she had recurring dreams of Aiden chasing her. Trying her best to shake off the feeling of dread that had taken hold of her nerves since his text, she got ready for the final day of the conference. Even though it was the last day, it actually ended at noon, so she had some free time to herself in the afternoon. Today she had plans to finish the sessions strong, then have lunch with Diane to say goodbye. After that, she had wanted to stroll through the city and do some light shopping by herself.

Stepping into the nearest taxicab, she made her way to the conference. She was still feeling anxiety over the Aiden situation. She hoped he was bluffing, and he wouldn't show up on her vacation. He liked to get under her skin with empty threats when she was back in Seattle, but she didn't know how far he'd go when she wasn't in his city.

The air was warmer today, but the atmosphere seemed to threaten colder weather as the day went on. She would enjoy the cooler weather as she shopped later on, working up a sweat walking around the city.

The conference center was almost empty when she got there. She hadn't been to many conferences before, but the small ones she had been to always tended to be sparse for attendees on the last day. Most people had the preference to get started on their journeys home after breakfast, choosing to forego the last of the sessions for an earlier seat in the airport, or lighter traffic on the roads.

Charlotte was excited that she could enjoy the last few hours of the conference and then start her vacation. She was even more excited to be able to partially share her vacation with Callum.

As she settled into the first session of the day, coffee and notebook in hand, she decided to check her phone. She had two messages, one from Diane and one from Callum. Good, she thought, nothing from Aiden. She clicked open Callum's message first.

MORNING BEAUTIFUL. SEE YOU TONIGHT. CAN'T WAIT. C.

The text was short and to the point, but it made her blush at the thought of what tonight could bring. She opened the message from Diane.

CAN'T WAIT FOR LUNCH. MEET OUTSIDE CONFERENCE CENTER AT NOON.

Charlotte typed out replies to both messages and hit send, putting the phone back in lap so she could periodically check messages during any lull in the session.

·········

As the last session of the conference finished, Charlotte felt like she knew what she needed to know about the new software to really get a head start on being a good leader for her team back home. She had planned to take a day or two of her vacation to write up some notes on her laptop and integrate them into a training plan for the rest of the team. The software implementation started as soon as she would get back to Seattle and she wanted to be prepared to hit the ground running. The College Dean was starting her trial period when she got back, so she felt like being here was really the head start that she needed to win the permanent promotion.

Looking around, she saw Diane coming toward her with a big smile on her face.

"Ready for lunch? I'm starving after all that learning!" Charlotte still couldn't believe how such a tiny frame was able to eat so much and yet still have such an amazing figure.

"Sure, let's go back to the cute bakery across the street." Charlotte had been meaning to go back and try a different pastry from there, plus their sandwiches were amazing.

"Fine by me, let's go!"

The two crossed the street and made their way to the bakery. Charlotte followed Diane to a seat by the window, putting their things down to claim the table among the lunch time rush, they then lined up to order. Both deciding to have a sandwich and a pastry, their food was soon ready, and they were able to quickly sit back at their table.

"So, what did you enjoy most about the conference?"

Charlotte thought hard about the question, images of Callum coming into her mind,

"Definitely learning about the different types of software we can use in University settings, how about you?"

"I went to a great session about administration software!"

"What time do you have to leave?" Charlotte wondered if maybe Diane would have time to go shopping with her after all.

"Right after lunch, actually. I want to get home as quick as I can and decompress before I get back to work. You're staying for vacation, right?"

"Yes, I'm so glad I decided to stay. Callum is showing me around a little bit, starting tonight actually."

"Ooooh, that's awesome! Are you guys a thing?"

"I'm not sure, not officially, but there's definitely something there. He's so…" Charlotte wasn't sure how to finish her sentence to adequately describe how Callum made her feel, she wasn't even sure she wanted to admit it to herself.

"Dreamy? Haha." Diane chuckled.

"Yeah I guess, haha."

"It's been so nice to make a friend on this trip. I hope we can keep in touch."

"Absolutely! You have my number!"

The two finished up their lunch and said their goodbyes outside of the bakery. Charlotte felt sad to have to say goodbye, but really quite glad to have made an unexpected friend while she was on vacation. She hadn't expected to meet anyone, and the time she'd spend with Diane was such fun. She would definitely miss her as she continued her vacation.

Charlotte made her way into the center of Edinburgh and started window shopping. There were the typical shops you would find on a high street, clothes shops, perfume shops, the usual phone shops and quaint little cafes. Dotted in between the typical shops were beautiful little boutiques selling different family and clan tartans, or little souvenir shops that Charlotte spent a long time looking through. She bought a few items to take home with her for friends and family, as well as some little things for herself as keepsakes.

Enjoying the time alone and finding the scenery relaxing, she carried on walking down the main street, contemplating stopping in one of the cafes for some coffee and a chance to rest. As she window shopped, she came across an interesting whiskey shop. Charlotte loved whiskey after being introduced to it by a former boyfriend back in Seattle, still, whiskey from the home of whiskey was something different altogether.

She pushed open the small door to the whiskey shop and stopped to inhale the warm scent of the shop. She took her time perusing each shelf before she found a cute miniature set, all in glass bottles and notes about the type, texture and tastes. She picked it up and took it to the counter with another few items that she hoped could fit in her suitcase. After she paid for her purchases, she decided that getting some coffee in one of the local cafes was a great idea.

Stepping into the nearest cafe, Charlotte ordered a large coffee and settled down by the window with her purchases. As she waited for her coffee to cool down, she looked through her purchases, examining each item in turn and feeling fascinated by the culture that surrounded her. Edinburgh was truly a beautiful city, and the whiskey was a completely different experience than she'd had back in Seattle.

The sound of the door opening caught Charlotte's attention. She looked up and saw a familiar sight entering the cafe. Callum. Their eyes locked at the same time and shared a smile.

"Is this seat taken?" He continued to smile down at her.

"It is now…"

"I thought I'd have to wait until this afternoon to get to see you." He sat close to her at the cafe table.

"Ah well I guess it's your lucky day."

"It sure is." Charlotte blushed and took a sip of her coffee.

"So, if you're not doing anything, what's say we start our trip early?"

"Oh? I need to grab my suitcase from the hotel."

"I can drop you off after the coffee, I thought it might be good to get a head start on our drive to the countryside."

"Ok! That sounds wonderful!"

Charlotte and Callum finished up their drinks and made their way to his car. They drove in a comfortable silence to Charlotte's hotel. When Callum pulled up to the entrance, she jumped out.

"I won't be long. Pretty much everything is packed already."

"Do you need help?"

"No, I got it." Charlotte hurried to pack her bathroom things, some cute outfits, and her make-up. She left the rest in the hotel drawers; she'd be back in a few days to finish up the rest of her vacation there.

Before she left the hotel, Charlotte let the reception desk know that she would be spending a few days in the countryside and to leave her hotel room for when she returned.

Hauling her suitcase into the back of Callum's car, she hopped back into the passenger seat.

"Hey, I could've put your case in the car."

"I got it, I'm stronger than I look."

Callum leant over to kiss Charlotte. Heat rose into her cheeks as she returned the kiss, opening her mouth to allow him deeper access. She moaned slightly as he probed her with his tongue. Pulling away, Callum looked almost sleepy with lust as he moved his tongue over his own lips.

"Let's get going, shall we?" Callum lazily drew out the words, making Charlotte want to climb into his lap. She moistened her lips.

"Where exactly are we going?"

"A little village called Linlithgow. It's about an hour's drive from here. It has this amazing loch and canal I want to show you, and some really interesting history too." Callum seemed excited as he spoke about his beautiful country.

"It sounds perfect. I can't wait to see it with you."
Charlotte settled into the leather seat as Callum
expertly turned the car back onto the main road. She
felt amazingly comfortable with this man she hadn't
long met and hoped the place they were going was
just as romantic as he made it sound. Then again, with
his thick Scottish accent, handsome good looks, and
strong body, almost anywhere seemed romantic by
his side.

....

9.

As they drove, Callum snuck a peek at Charlotte. Her head was gently resting against the window with her arms wrapped around herself. Her long, wavy, brown hair was partially covering her face. She was gently purring in her sleep. Smiling to himself, he couldn't quite believe the emotions he had for this woman, a woman who just a few short days ago he'd never even met.

When she'd bumped into him in that first coffee shop and he couldn't get her out of his mind, he knew they shared something special. He tried to remind himself that she was only here for a week or so longer. He knew he shouldn't get attached, but deep down, awareness spread through him and he realized it wouldn't be that easy to let her go.

....

The feel of bumpy roads woke Charlotte from her sleep. She couldn't remember when exactly she'd dropped off, but she must've needed the nap. Stretching in her seat, she looked out of the window to the magnificent views of stone architecture all around her. They were driving over a cobblestone bridge and into the town. In the distance, Charlotte could see a body of water, she hoped they would get to visit, it looked so peaceful.

"We're almost there", Callum smiled at her from the drivers' seat.

"What's the town called, again? Lin…?"

"Linlithgow. It's in the West Lothian part of Scotland."

"It's so old looking, the views are beautiful."

"Yes, it's one of the oldest towns we have, full of rich history. I can't wait to show you around, let's find where we're staying first."

Callum pulled further into the town and Charlotte continued to look out of her window, awed at the town and the history that it must have witnessed.

They parked in a small parking lot close to the huge body of water Charlotte had seen from the bridge. She remembered Callum telling her earlier that it was a Loch. Pulling their bags out of the car, Callum came to stand beside her, both looking out over the water.

"It's beautiful isn't it?" His scent filled the air next to her and she stopped breathing for a second.

"It really is. We should get a picnic there while we're here."

"Great idea. Here, let's get checked into the hotel."

The two walked over to a hotel overlooking the Loch. Charlotte hoped they would get a window view; she couldn't imagine taking her eyes off the serene waterfront.

Callum checked them into the hotel. It was more of an inn than a hotel. It was small but had obviously been renovated. It felt homely, but at the same time it had modern features that blended into the history of the building. There was a small bar with tables and chairs off to one side with a giant hearth fireplace. Tartan covered the floors in a rich blue shade that made her feel proud to be in this country. Charlotte could imagine how nice it would be to cozy up next to the fireplace with some whiskey on a cold night. She really loved it here, not just in this town, but in Scotland. She would really hate to leave next week.

"Ready?" Callum signaled her to follow up the stairs to the room.

Entering the hotel room, Charlotte thought how quaint it was, but still modern. The bed looked so comfortable. She couldn't wait to share it with Callum, though she imagined sleeping was the last thing they would be doing. Checking out the bathroom, Charlotte loved the soft finishings in there, and though it was small, it still managed to be light and airy. There was a claw foot tub that she couldn't wait to use, as she wondered whether she would fit in there with Callum, he came up behind her and put his arms around her waist.

"What do you think?" he whispered into her ear.

"I think it's perfect", she turned around to face him. He cupped her face with one hand and pulled her closer for a kiss with the other.

"Why don't we check out the bed?" He was almost growling by the time they actually made it to the bed.

....

"That was amazing", Charlotte could have easily fallen asleep in Callum's arms, but she was eager to explore the town before they lost the daylight.

"Can we go and explore?" She nudged Callum as he tried to sleep.

"Mmmhmm, let's go."

"What do you want to see first?" Callum laughed lightly as Charlotte pulled a visitor's brochure from her bag. She'd picked it up on the way out of the hotel.

"There's a palace here?!" She gasped and looked up at Callum.

"Aye, very old, very big, not what you think of though when you think palace. It's right up this hill."

The two walked up to the palace slowly. Charlotte put away her brochure. There seemed to be a lot of activities in the town, but really, she was content to be walking around with Callum. As if he read her mind, his hand found hers as they were walking and squeezed. She wondered if he felt the same. She also wondered how he felt about her leaving in a week. Pushing the thought to the back of her mind, she tried to ignore the swell of worry that began in the pit of her stomach. She would enjoy these few days with Callum and forget for a minute that it had to come to an end.

The sound of her stomach growling interrupted her thoughts. She hadn't eaten since they'd left for the drive to Linlithgow.

"Hey, let's get something to eat, I'm starving!" She looked hopefully at Callum.

"Sure, I know just the place."

....

After they'd eaten, Callum and Charlotte spent hours walking around the palace and the Loch, hand in hand, just two content lovers.

"Do you think there were many romances at the palace? You know, couples doing the same thing as us?" Charlotte realized she sounded dreamy, but she couldn't help herself around Callum.

"Well, I'm not sure about romances exactly, but Mary Queen of Scots was born in this castle!"

"Oh wow, really?! Did she have a romantic life?"

"Uh, not exactly. She had two marriages that didn't end well, or so they say."

"Oh."

Carrying on in silence, the pair started to turn back when Charlotte's phone vibrated in her pocket, startling her.

"Oh, my phone. One sec." She reached into her pocket to see who was messaging her.

I'M HERE. WHERE ARE YOU?

Charlotte's blood ran cold and her heart almost stopped in her chest. Aiden was here? In Scotland.

WHY ARE YOU HERE? IT'S MY VACATION.

She hurriedly typed out a response.

"Is everything alright? You've got white as a sheet!" Charlotte looked up into Callum's worried eyes. Should she tell him? She didn't want to ruin their trip.

"Uh, no, nothing, I'm fine." She put her phone back in her pocket, glad that she'd stepped away from Edinburgh for a few days.

"Let's head back to the hotel and warm up by the fire."

"That sounds perfect." Charlotte wanted to enjoy her time with Callum but felt that she would need to deal with Aiden as soon as possible. Why had he come all this way? She didn't understand why he wouldn't just leave her alone to her vacation, or alone in general. Even when they were in Seattle, he constantly bothered her.

Charlotte and Callum made their way back to the hotel, taking their time to enjoy the final few minutes of sunset before they stepped into the warm and cozy hotel for the night. Charlotte couldn't wait to be alone with Callum, away from passersby and other couples.

....

Sipping the warm whiskey and settling deeper into an overstuffed chair, Charlotte languished in the heat coming off the fireplace. By the time they had entered the hotel, it had started to get quite cold outside. She was glad of the combined heat from the strong alcohol and the high flames coming off the fireplace.

Sitting opposite her, Callum studied Charlotte from behind his own whiskey glass. He had wondered what had changed her attitude during their walk around the palace. At first, she was almost serene as they walked hand in hand and chatted about the history of the town, but then she got that text message. Ever since, she'd been looking over her shoulder, anxious, almost expecting someone to pop up.

Callum wasn't sure if he should question her about it, or whether he should let her come to him in her own time. He didn't want to push her but at the same time he had an unshakable urge to protect her and keep her safe from whatever it was that made her look over her shoulder every time someone's chair moved against the wood floors.

"Charlotte, is something bothering you... you seem, off, maybe." He didn't want to push it, but he needed her to feel safe with him, to relax.

"Uh, yes, no, no, I'm fine, just tired." He knew that wasn't it but didn't push.

"Shall we head to bed?" Smiling at her, he sensed her ease a little as she nodded.

Taking their almost empty glasses to the bar, Callum thanked the barkeeper and led Charlotte upstairs.

"If anything was bothering you, if you were worried about anything, you can always tell me. I'm here for you Charlotte, for as long as you need." His admission had slipped out before he had a chance to engage his better judgements, but what he said was true, and from the heart. He wanted to protect this woman.

Instead of replying, Charlotte smiled up at him. She didn't know what to say, or how to say it. She didn't know if she should tell him about Aiden. Besides, she'd be back in Seattle soon and Callum couldn't protect her from there. She had to keep her head down, try to deal with Aiden as best she could and try to enjoy the last few days, she had with Callum, and with Scotland. She just hoped Aiden wouldn't ruin the time she did have left here.

Charlotte felt sad as she settled into bed with Callum. She couldn't shake the worry she had at Aiden's message. She hadn't checked her phone again; she didn't want to face that reality until she was back in Edinburgh. He would have known she would be somewhere there because of the conference, work would have told him where it was. There was no way he could know she was here though, she hadn't told anyone. He would never think to come to this town, an hour outside of the capitol. That thought let her feel safe as she snuggled further into Callum's arms and drifted into a deep sleep.

....

10.

"NO, NO, STOP, PLEASE."

"Charlotte! Wake up, wake up. It's just a dream."
Callum's soothing voice cut through her nightmare.

"Oh, I'm sorry. I had a nightmare." Embarrassed for
her sleep-induced outburst, Charlotte felt her cheeks
begin to redden.

"Are you alright? Do you want to talk about it?"
Settling back into the sheets, Callum turned her to
face him and put a comforting arm around her waist.

"Just... "Charlotte didn't know whether or not to tell
Callum about Aiden. Maybe if she watered it down it
would be ok.

"You can tell me, it's ok."

"The text message I got yesterday, the one you asked
about? It was from someone from back in Seattle. We
kind of work together, he's the one trying to push the
College Dean away from giving me the promotion.
Well, he's here in Scotland. I guess he didn't want me
to stay past the conference dates and decided to pay
me a visit."

"How odd, why would he come here like that?"

"I mean, I don't know, I'm only guessing. He um… I mean, him and I. We have a history. Not a very nice history either. Maybe he thought he could bring me home. I haven't spoken to him. He doesn't know I'm here; he thinks I'm in Edinburgh or something. I told him I was taking vacation, but I guess he didn't like that."

"Charlotte, are you frightened of this man?" Callum seemed concerned. He pulled her a little closer but kept his grip light on her waist.

"Uh, no, yes, I don't know. Sometimes he can be a little forceful. Like I said, we have history, and some of it is ugly. But it's not all his fault."

"Has he ever hurt you?" Charlotte could tell Callum wanted to push more, but she just didn't want to be having this conversation, at least, not until she'd dealt with Aiden.

"Callum… Let's not talk about this right now. Please?" She pulled the sheets further up to her chin and hid her head beneath Callum's.

"Ok, it's alright. You're always safe with me."

Charlotte ducked out from under Callum's chin. She gently kissed him. Callum kissed her back gently and pulled her body closer to his. Her kiss became more and more urgent as he kissed her back. Suddenly, he broke off the kiss and she felt cold where his lips had left her."

"Are you sure you want to do this?" Callum needed her badly, he couldn't explain why, but he just knew in his heart, soul and body that he needed to claim her right now. He couldn't though, not until he knew she was ok, not when he thought she'd been hurt by another man.

"Yes, please Callum, I need you."

That was all the confirmation he needed to pull her back to him and kiss her again. Each kiss became more urgent as they both deepened the kiss. With every thrust of his tongue, Charlotte moaned and writhed her body over his, needing to feel him inside her, needing that sweet release only he could bring her.

Pushing the covers aside, Callum gently pushed Charlotte onto her back. He hungrily shuffled down the bed until he was face to face with her center. She was naked from the waist up, a thin layer of black lace all that separated him from his meal. Dipping his finger underneath the lace, he cupped her swollen apex until she bucked underneath him.

"Please..." She was breathless beneath his touch, which only made his arousal more painful.

Slowly, Callum slid his fingers into her, feeling the warmth spread over his fingers as she groaned. He couldn't stand it any longer, he had to taste her. Bending his head to use his mouth to replace his hand, he devoured her until she begged him to stop.

Pushing up off his bulging biceps, he claimed her with one big thrust. Sending waves of pleasure rippling through both of their bodies. As she started to cry out, he captured her mouth and felt her cry inside of his body. Thrust after thrust, he pushed into her, needing to feel her, needing her to feel him as they came together. Callum didn't want to let go, instead, he remained inside her as he tightened his grip on her, not wanting to break their union.

Charlotte let out a satisfied purr and pushed his arm closer to her. She must be feeling the same way as Callum because she didn't let go for a long time either.

....

Sometime later, Charlotte and Callum woke again. They had been making love for hours, neither one wanting to let go of the other, caught in a time loop of pleasure.

"Mmm, I guess we should get up." Callum was resting on Charlotte's head, so at first, she wasn't sure if she had said that or if he had.

"Let's get breakfast. I'm starved."

"I hate to tell you this, but it's closer to lunch time." Callum looked at his watch and chuckled.

"Ok, now we definitely need to get up. This is our last day in Linlithgow!"

Charlotte rolled off the bed and padded to the shower. She stepped into the cold water to wake herself up. As the shower heated up, Callum came in behind her. It was a tight fit, but she didn't mind being this close to him.

Grabbing the shower puff, Callum poured liquid soap on top and dipped it into the warm stream of water. Slowly, he went over every inch of Charlotte's body, stopping when he reached her breasts. She turned her head to face him and he caught her mouth in a kiss at the same time as he lightly pinched her nipple with his free hand. She let out a lazy moan and continued to kiss him. He dropped the shower puff and used his hands to move lather across her body.

When he got to her center, he teased her clitoris with a single finger, making her back arch against his front. His penis grew hard against her buttocks. Pulling her face to his, he kissed her, then used his free hand to place each of her hands against the wall of the shower. The cold tile against the heat of Callum's body threatened to send her over the edge. He resumed teasing her clitoris with one hand, bracing himself with the other against the cold tile of the shower wall. He thrust gently inside her, sending them both over the edge in seconds. He turned her around to face him and kissed her once more.

"You're so beautiful." He whispered under the roaring shower water, just loud enough for her to hear. She blushed slightly and smiled up at him.

Finishing their shower, they stepped out of the hot water at the same time, wrapping themselves in fluffy towels. Charlotte decided she wouldn't bother with make-up; she was too hungry. The two got dressed quickly and made their way out of the hotel room.

"Why don't we get that picnic?" Callum had remembered that Charlotte wanted to eat by the Loch before she left the town.

"Yes! I would love that."

"I know a place in town we can go to grab the supplies."

The two stepped into a local deli, inside were heavy tables lining each wall, with a quaint counter at the end of the room, with meats and cheeses lining the chiller. Callum ordered for them, choosing two fresh bread loaves, olives, and a selection of meats and cheeses. The lady behind the counter carefully packed up their items and handed them to Charlotte.

As they walked hand in hand to the Loch, Charlotte's stomach began to growl. She couldn't wait to tuck into all the delicious fresh food from the deli.

"This looks like a good spot." Callum sat down on a wooden bench and motioned for Charlotte to sit next to him.

Charlotte carefully took each of the small packages out of the bag she carried from the deli. Each package was still warm and smelled wonderful. Her stomach growled again, which made Callum laugh.

Callum pulled out one of the bread loaves. He pulled it apart and handed one piece to Charlotte. Opening two of the little pots that had been in the deli bag, he smeared butter, then mayonnaise on his and Charlotte's piece of bread, then motioned for her to pile some cheese meats and olives onto her piece. Charlotte brought the sandwich to her mouth, almost drooling at the smell coming from the combination of ingredients and moaned gently as she chewed and swallowed.

"Good, right?" Callum was grinning at her from under his own sandwich.

"Oh my God, this is the best thing I've ever tasted."

"That's because you've worked up quite the appetite." Callum grinned sheepishly at her. Charlotte couldn't help but grin back.

....

"Callum? Callum! It is you!" An older man was walking over to where Charlotte and Callum sat overlooking the Loch. He was tall, even taller than Callum, with white hair and a matching, but trimmed, white beard. He spoke with a gentle Scottish accent.

"Dean Campbell! Nice to see you here!" Callum stood and greeted the older gentleman.

"And who might this be?" Dean Campbell extended his hand to Charlotte. She stood up and shook his hand.

"I'm Charlotte, pleased to meet you."

"Are you two in town long? When are you headed back to Edinburgh?"

"We leave tomorrow, how about you? Needed a break from the city too, huh?" Callum spoke easily with the older man, which put her at ease with him too.

"We go back in a week. My wife and I decided to take some time away from the bustle. You should join us for supper tonight, that is, if you don't already have plans?"

"We'd love to! If that's alright with you?" Charlotte nodded up at Callum, it would be nice to dine with another couple.

"Who's he?" When the man had walked away, making plans to meet with them later that evening, Charlotte couldn't resist finding more about him.

"That is Dean Campbell, he oversees one of the departments at the University of Edinburgh, where I teach. He's been working on a few projects with me, but we aren't in the same department. He's housed over in Business, but I'm in the English department for teaching. Actually, he would be a good contact for you! He worked on the software creation with me."

"Oh, that's great! I can't wait to pick his brains at supper!"

"I'm sure he'd enjoy that!" Callum smiled down at Charlotte.

"Let's walk around the Loch!" Charlotte was full from lunch and wanted to walk off some of her excitement at meeting Dean Campbell.

....

.

11.

"Are you almost ready?" Callum was standing at the bathroom entrance in their hotel room.

"Yeah, just about. I just need to get some clothes on."

"Must you? I think you look great like that…"
Callum looked her up and down with a hungry look
on his face. Charlotte knew it wasn't because he was
hungry for food.

"I'm sure Dean Campbell and his wife would
disagree."

"Mmmhmm…" Charlotte didn't think Callum was
listening. She bit her lip and looked him in the eye.

"That lip bite again…" In two short strides, Callum
reached Charlotte and pulled her to him. He killed her
neck and spoke close to her ear.

"Callum…" she couldn't remember what she was
going to say. He had a way of taking her thoughts
away with a single kiss.

"Mmm?"

"We'll be late…" Callum stepped away and she felt
cold where the heat of his breath had left her neck.

"You better get dressed before I make us really damn
late." Callum laughed and backed into the bedroom.

Charlotte came into the bedroom and looked through her suitcase. She wanted to wear something professional, yet sexy. She found a cute red dress that clung to her curves but was forgiving enough to eat a big meal with. She stood back up and saw Callum watching her from the bed. He was already dressed in navy slacks and a crisp white button-down shirt. He'd left the top few buttons undone, allowing Charlotte a view of the top of his chest hair. Charlotte couldn't wait to run her hands through it when they were alone in bed.

Dropping her bath towel, Charlotte laughed as Callum groaned and fell to the bed. She quickly dressed and came to sit next to him to put her black heeled sandals on.

"Ok, I'm ready. I'm dressed. You can look now." Charlotte laughed down as Callum still laid on the bed with his eyes closed, his legs over the end of the bed.

"Alright, let's go before I lose my restraint. You make me lose my mind."

"Ha, I'm not the only one buster!"

....

Charlotte was awed as she entered the Italian restaurant in the town. Callum held the door open for her and she thanked him with a smile as she stepped into the warmth of the restaurant. The smell of garlic and homemade marinara sauce filled the air. The walls were lined with giant, gothic mirrors and heavy tables sat at angles inside the restaurant. It was dark inside the restaurant, so it took Charlotte a minute to find their dining partners.

Callum came up behind her, spotting his friends at the same time as Charlotte.

"Dean Campbell! There you are." Callum called over to his friend.

"Please, Callum, how many times do I need to tell you to call me Bernard?"

"At least once more, friend."

"Come, sit with us." Bernard motioned to a table nearby.

"This is my wife, Aileen. Callum I believe you've met before."

"Just the once, nice to see you again, Aileen. This is my girlfriend, Charlotte."

"Girlfriend, huh?" Charlotte whispered quietly.

"Nice to meet you, Aileen, and lovely to see you again Dean Campbell." Charlotte reached to shake the hands of their companions as they sat down at the table.

Bernard ordered wine and water for the table. As the servers brought the wine to the table, Charlotte reveled in the gentle glug of her glass being filled. Bread and oil were placed on the table with large menus for each of the four.

"There's so much to choose from." Charlotte couldn't decide what she wanted.

"You can't go wrong with the homemade marinara dishes, dearie." Aileen smiled over at Charlotte. She was an older woman, with kind brown eyes. She was quite beautiful, and her warm smile made Charlotte wonder what she would have looked like when she was younger.

After the waiter took their orders, Charlotte took a sip of her wine. It was strong, but smooth, with a sweet aftertaste. She settled into her chair just as Bernard looked over to her.

"So, Charlotte, what brings you to Scotland?" Bernard seemed curious.

"I came for a conference, but it ended a few days ago. I've taken a couple of extra weeks here so I can enjoy the country."

"Ah lovely, did you learn much from your conference?"

"I did! Actually, I really came to learn about the software you and Callum worked on. It's a crucial part of a promotion I'm trying to win at work."

"Oh? And where is that work?"

"I work for the University of Seattle. I'm in admin at the moment, but since I finished my MBA, I really wanted to work to lead a team in the Business School. Part of the promotion process is to lead a team to implement a new software for the college."

"And that software just so happens to be the one Callum and I developed? Well, if we can help you in any way, please let me know."

"And are you enjoying Scotland, dearie?" Aileen took a chance to step into the conversation.

"Very much! I really don't want to leave." Charlotte looked over at Callum, not wanting to imagine leaving him.

"So why don't you stay?" Bernard was looking at her with an expression she couldn't discern.

"I uh… I didn't think that was an option." Could she stay? What about the promotion?

"Tell me, this promotion, is it something you want because it's in Seattle, or would you consider a similar position here in Edinburgh?"

"Oh, I can't say I've thought about it. I do enjoy Seattle, but it isn't where I would consider home."

"Where do you consider home? Do you not have family back in Seattle?"

"Actually, my parents live in Europe and I'm an only child. They moved there for my mother's work as a surgeon and I stayed in Seattle. I don't know that I've really found a place to call home, at least not yet." Charlotte wasn't sure why she was sharing so much, but the older couple seemed almost like grandparents to her.

"Perhaps before your vacation ends you might find that feeling of home."

Charlotte smiled at Bernard. She wasn't sure that she could stay here, there wasn't a job for her, nor a place to stay. Plus, she had the promotion to think about, she had wanted it, hadn't she? She knew she didn't want to work in her admin job anymore, and she definitely wanted to use her MBA, but at the University of Seattle? She'd applied because it was easier, she already worked there, and Aiden had pushed her to apply.

Their meal arrived and they ate quietly. Charlotte concentrated on her meal while Callum and Bernard talked about work, and Aileen made small talk with her. She was deep in thought by the time the dessert menu came.

"Oh Charlotte, you must try the tiramisu! It's divine!" Aileen was excited as she thumbed through the small menu.

"Well, if everyone else is! Though, you may need to roll me back to the hotel." Charlotte looked at Callum expecting him to laugh at her joke, instead she found an expression on his face she couldn't make out. He seemed deep in thought, she wasn't sure if he'd even heard her.

Bernard ordered a different wine as they put in their orders for dessert. Charlotte was excited to try the new wine; Bernard has exquisite taste if the last one was anything to go by.

When the dessert came, Charlotte took her first bite of tiramisu and moaned aloud. Luckily, only Callum seemed to have heard her.

"Do that again and I won't be able to hide my erection." Callum leant over to whisper into her ear, making her close her eyes.

"I'm not sure if it's the wine or the food, but I'm feeling sleepy. I don't know that I'll be all that... energetic to keep up with your erection tonight." She whispered back.

"Mmm, maybe we'll just have to take it slow tonight." She looked up to see Callum smiling softly at her. There was a look in his eye other than hunger for her. He blinked and his expression changed, but Charlotte could have sworn she saw something else there... love.

....

"Charlotte, I'd like you to visit my office at the University of Edinburgh sometime before you leave. I'd like to show you our space, and perhaps give you a chance to use the software." Bernard spoke loudly, probably because of the wine, as they stood up to leave.

"I'd love that!"

"Aileen and I will be back in the city in a little under a week. Callum can make the arrangements for you to visit when we return."

The group said their goodbyes and left the restaurant. Charlotte felt giddy with the combination of good food, good wine, and the excitement of getting her hands on more than just a demo of the software. This opportunity would put her ahead in her promotion prospects, if that was still what she even wanted. Bernard's words played in her mind and she wondered whether or not she would find a place to call home, somewhere she felt like she belonged. She definitely didn't feel that way in Seattle, not with Aiden always on her tail. Aiden. She'd momentarily forgotten that he was back in Edinburgh. She hoped she could deal with him and make him leave. She'd have to face him sooner or later.

Unlocking the door to the hotel and pushing it open, Callum motioned for Charlotte to enter the room. When she turned around, Callum was smiling at her.

"Would you stay?" He looked hopeful.

"I didn't know it was an option. I'm not sure. My job is in Seattle."

"Your job yes, but what if you had a job here. What if you could stay here, with me?"

"I… I'm not sure. It's so beautiful here, and you… you make me feel…"

Before she could finish her sentence, Callum had closed the gap between them and was kissing her gently. She didn't want to entertain the thought that she might be able to stay for fear that her hopes would be dashed when she had to leave. Deep down, she knew she didn't want to leave Callum, that it would be the hardest thing she'd ever done.

"I think I'm going to have a bath before bed." She turned to Callum as they got into the hotel room.

"May I join you?"

"I'd like that very much."

"Wait here." Callum sat Charlotte on the bed and walked to the bathroom.

He came back a few minutes later and beckoned Charlotte to come with him into the bathroom.

"Wow, all this just for me?" Charlotte looked around at the candles dimly lighting the bathroom and bubbles peeking from the top of a steaming bath.

She stepped into the warm tub and sighed as she sat beneath the bubbles. Callum slid in behind her, pulling her close to him. Charlotte leaned against him and relaxed into the bath while Callum soaped up her body.

"Charlotte?" Callum whispered softly in her ear. She'd fallen asleep against him.

"Mmm?"

He gently pulled her up to stand, rinsing her off, and wrapped an oversized towel around her body. Lifting her from the bathtub, he carried her to the bed and laid her softly down.

Getting into bed, she snuggled as close to Callum as she could. She needed to feel him close for fear of losing him. She was realizing that the more time she spent with him, the less she wanted to go back to Seattle.

....

12.

The drive back to Edinburgh seemed quicker than the drive out to Linlithgow. Charlotte felt truly relaxed, both in the company of Callum, and from their trip to the countryside. She was anxious to get back to the city and deal with the Aiden situation. Given his history, she wouldn't be surprised if he was playing with her and he wasn't even here at all.

"You seem deep in thought." Callum's soft voice brought her from thoughts of Aiden and into the real world.

"Just thinking about getting back to Edinburgh, we're close, aren't we?"

"We are, maybe ten minutes out, another five or so to your hotel. Tell me, are you thinking about that guy?"

"Aiden? Yeah. If he really is in the city, I'll need to deal with him."

"Do you need me to be there when you do?"

"No, no, it's something I need to do myself. I'll just see why he's here. Maybe the University didn't want me to take vacation, though they approved it, so I'm not sure why he'd come all this way."

They drove the rest of the way in silence, Callum not sure what to say, and Charlotte anxious to be back in the city. They had both had such a romantic time away together, and yet the threat of Aiden's visit seemed to hang between them, changing the atmosphere.

Callum pulled up to the hotel grounds and stopped the car. He turned to Charlotte with an unreadable expression on his face.

"When can I see you again?" He smiled sheepishly.

"We just got back after two days together." She smiled back at him.

"I can't get enough of you, Charlotte. And you're leaving at the end of this week. I want to spend as much time as I can with you, if you'd like."

"I would, of course I would. I'm just teasing you."

"Have coffee with me tomorrow afternoon? I have class all morning."

"I'd love to. How about the coffee shop where we met, where I bumped into you for the first time?"

"Sounds ideal. I'll see you at 2pm."

....

It was mid-morning when Charlotte and Callum returned to Edinburgh. She had a quick refreshing shower and changed into jeans and a sweater. She opened her laptop and checked her emails for the first time since she had got to Edinburgh, there was nothing out of the ordinary, just usual work emails. She quickly replied to them all and opened her private emails. One from Dean Campbell was among the top few.

Charlotte opened the email at once, excited to see his name in her mailbox. The email was another invitation to come and see him in two days' time. He and his wife had cut their visit to Linlithgow short, but the email didn't say why. Perhaps one of them had business in the city that needed attending to. Charlotte replied that she would meet him in his office two days from now and asked if there was anything in particular, she should bring. Shutting down her laptop, she suddenly had the urge for a coffee and a pastry, and perhaps some more shopping.

....

Charlotte slipped into a taxicab outside of the hotel and asked to be taken to the city center. She slowly wandered around the streets of Edinburgh, dipping in and out of shops until she came across a cafe that she hadn't previously seen.

The door was open and welcoming with the smell of freshly brewed coffee coming through the doorway. Charlotte stepped inside and walked up to the counter. Pastries, pasta pots and sandwiches lined up in the glass cabinet, chalk menus lined the walls behind the counter, offering various flavors of teas and coffees. After all the walking and lovemaking, she'd done over the past few days, she decided to treat herself to a feast.

Taking her packages and coffee cup to one of the tables by the window, Charlotte laid out her feast and jumped up onto one of the high chairs. She'd chosen a pasta pot, pastry and black coffee to indulge herself as she people watched through the window. Taking a deep breath, she really felt at home here in Edinburgh. Not for the first time, Charlotte was beginning to wish there was a way for her to stay here. As if reading her mind, her phone buzzed with a message from Callum.

I MISS YOU ALREADY. C x

I MISS YOU TOO x

Charlotte replied almost immediately. The messages sending butterflies to her stomach.

WORKING LATE TONIGHT AT WORK. CAN'T WAIT TO SEE YOU TOMORROW x

DON'T WORK TOO HARD! SEE YOU TOMORROW x

Her phone buzzed again, but this time it was an email. Dean Campbell had replied to her message asking her to bring her resume if she had one to hand. Charlotte had her resume on her computer, she wondered if the hotel had a place for her to print it off. She would need to remember to ask at the reception desk when she got back to the hotel.

Finishing off her lunch, Charlotte decided to do some more shopping in the city before heading back to the hotel.

Stepping into a big-name lingerie shop, Charlotte felt her stomach flip in excitement and anticipation as she fingered the delicate silks and lace of the underwear sets. She had decided that she would buy something special for the next time she would see Callum. She couldn't wait to see the look on his face when he undressed her and found her hiding sexy underwear underneath her clothes.

She tried on a few items, not able to decide which she preferred better. Deciding to buy two different sets as a treat, she took them to the counter and felt excitement rise from her stomach to her cheeks as the lady wrapped up the garments in tissue paper and put them into a bag.

Checking her phone, Charlotte realized it was getting a little late in the afternoon and she really wanted to see about getting a resume printed. She walked to the nearest taxicab rank and jumped into the first one waiting with her purchases bouncing behind her.

....

Back at the hotel, Charlotte stopped at the reception desk to ask about a printer.

"Ah yes, we certainly do. Incidentally, you also have a message. A young man, an American, came to see you while you were out. He left a message, just let me find it."

Oh God. It could only be Aiden. How had he found her here, and why had he come to the hotel?

"Here it is. Someone called Aiden said he would be back to see you tomorrow."

"Right, thank you." Charlotte felt herself go weak at the thought of Aiden being in her hotel.

The hotel receptionist motioned toward where the printers were kept next to two old looking computers. Charlotte went up to her room to fetch her laptop and came back down to print a few copies of her resume for her meeting with Dean Campbell. Going back to her room with the printouts, Charlotte rested on her bed for a second. Thoughts of Aiden ran through her head, giving her a headache. She laid down for a while and fell asleep.

....

The next morning, Charlotte woke up early. Feeling refreshed, she dressed herself in a set of the new silky lingerie she'd bought the day before and slipped a cotton dress over the top. Pulling her jacket over her shoulders and adding a light scarf, she was ready for the day. After checking her work emails, she'd decided to go and eat breakfast at the hotel buffet, which she had yet to do on her trip so far.

Charlotte made her way downstairs and walked toward the smell of fresh, though burnt, coffee. The breakfast area was small but bright. Food lined one wall, encased in clear plastic partitions, and a drinks table was laid out across another wall. Small cafe type tables were laid out in the middle of the room. Sitting down at a table in the back of the room, closest to the coffee pots, Charlotte wondered what she would try first. Deciding to eat light, she grabbed a coffee, some eggs and a piece of toast with butter.

"Good morning, miss." An older gentleman greeted her as he got his own breakfast.

"Good morning." She nodded and greeted him back. Charlotte wasn't good at early morning small talk.

Her phone buzzed with two messages. One from Callum, another from Aiden. She opened Callum's first.

SEE YOU AT 2! C x

Typing out a reply, she then opened the message from Aiden. Her nerves were on edge waiting for what he would say.

CAME TO YOUR HOTEL. NEED TO SEE YOU NOW. WHERE ARE YOU??

Charlotte replied, again asking him why he was here and what he wanted. When neither he nor Callum replied to her messages, she shoved her phone back in her bag.

....

When 2pm rolled around, Charlotte was already waiting inside the coffee shop for Callum. Checking her watch, she noted that he was running a little late. Pulling out her phone, she got ready to text him but stopped as she sensed him coming through the door. Looking up, their eyes locked, and a wide smile started on both of their faces.

"Hey beautiful." His words made Charlotte blush.

"Well hey there handsome."

"Let me grab us some coffees." Callum headed to the counter to order. She watched him as he strode easily back to their table clutching two coffee cups. He really was a sight for sore eyes. Her heart fluttered at the same time the butterflies in her stomach tripped over one another. She wouldn't admit it, but Charlotte was starting to have real feelings for this man.

....

13.

As the two chatted about everything and nothing, Charlotte felt her blood run cold as she heard a familiar voice in the background of the cafe. Aiden. Slowly, the color drained from her face and she turned around to face him. Her stomach was doing flips and she could barely breathe. A mix of fear and anxiety swirled in her mind. She felt Callum grab her hand. Turning to look at Callum, Charlotte couldn't make out what he was saying to her past the swirling she heard in her ears.

"Charlotte…" It was Callum who spoke, but it felt like he was in the distance when Charlotte tried to make her own voice work. She just looked at him, not sure what to do.

"Well, well, well. I should've known you'd be close to coffee. Found you at last." Aiden's thick American accent found its way down Charlotte's spine.

"Aiden." It was all she could muster.

"Who's your friend, Charlotte." The way he said her name was more like a curse than a greeting.

"Hi pal, my name's Callum, and who might you be?" The look on Callum's face told Charlotte that he'd already figured out who this man was.

"Aiden. Nice to meet ya. Mind telling me what you're doing looking all cozy." Aiden's voice was firm, angry.

"What's it to you pal?" Charlotte didn't recognize Callum's voice. She didn't know what to do, should she chime in?

"She's my wife!"

Charlotte felt the room go black; she dug her nails into the cafe chair to stop herself from passing out. She controlled her breathing until the world came back into focus. No-one was speaking, they were all looking at her.

"Charlotte… is this true? You're married?" Callum looked hurt, she couldn't bear it.

"Yes…. but…" Charlotte's voice came out in a whisper. Callum didn't give her the chance to finish her sentence before he was gone.

"Callum…" She called after him, but it was too late. He had already left the cafe.

"Looks like lover boy didn't like that, huh?" Aiden was grinning as he slid into the chair Callum just left.

"What are you doing here, Aiden?" Her voice was harsh, her heart hurting for Callum.

"I came to get you, Charlotte. Why are you here anyway? The conference you tricked the Dean into letting you attend ended days ago."

"I told you, I'm on vacation before my promotion starts, and I didn't trick anyone."

"Promotion? Ha! You don't stand a chance." Aiden almost spat the words at her.

"Aiden. Why did you come all this way?"

"I told you. I'm bringing you home. Let's get your things and get back to Seattle."

"No. I still have a few days left and you can't control me any more Aiden."

"Why? Because the last I saw, you need me, and that Scottish fella just left you here. He doesn't want you Charlotte, no-one does."

Charlotte wanted to cry, but she refused to waste the time she'd had away from him. She'd grown stronger in Edinburgh, and more like her old self, the Charlotte she was before she'd gotten involved with Aiden.

"Listen. We aren't together anymore Aiden. You have no say in my life."

"Ha. I have a say in whether or not you get that promotion. Do you want to stay in admin forever? You're nothing without me Charlotte."

"If it means being rid of you, yes. Leave me alone. Leave here. Go back to Seattle. I will never go with you."

"Then I'll have to make you. You'll be back on that plane to Seattle with or without me, but you will be back."

Charlotte sat shaking long after Aiden had left the cafe. She let a single tear roll down her cheek before she hardened herself. She wouldn't let him win. She would be her own person. She needed to get Callum to hear her out.

....

Charlotte had meant to head back to the hotel to decompress after her encounter with Callum, but instead she found herself walking around the Old Town of Edinburgh, fascinated by the gothic feel of the buildings.

She walked around for hours and hours, using the beautiful sights to clear her mind from the stresses of the day. The sun was starting to set as she realized she hadn't eaten since breakfast. Suddenly ravenous, she stopped into a local pub for some much-needed alcohol and something to fill the ache in her stomach. Charlotte had a feeling that the pain she was feeling was only partially to do with hunger.

Pushing the door to the pub open, she found a seat in the corner and waited for the server to take her order.

"What'll it be, miss?" A young lad, barely of drinking age, came to take her order.

"Um… Can I get a beer, actually, and whatever you recommend for a good hearty meal?" Charlotte didn't have the attention span to figure out what she wanted from the vast menu.

"Looking for some soul food are ya now?"

"Yes, please. Give me what you got." She smiled weakly as the server hurried off.

A little while later, he came back with a pint of lager and a plate of piping hot camembert with a bowl of various dipping foods. Charlotte's stomach growled as she dipped into the melty cheese.

"Don't fill up, that's just the starter, lass." A wicked grin spread across his face.

The food and ale helped to soothe Charlotte's soul, but she didn't know what to do about Callum, or Aiden. Aiden, she wanted to just ignore, but Callum. How could she make him understand? She'd sent him numerous messages and tried to call him, but each piece of communication had gone unanswered. She tried to put herself in his shoes, but she only came up hurt and angry that he wouldn't at least hear her out. She'd tried to tell him about Aiden.

Maybe she hadn't tried hard enough to explain her situation. She was feeling really sorry for herself when the server came back with a huge plate of food.

"Alright, dig in, lass. This is a toad in the hole."

"It smells wonderful!"

"I hope you enjoy it, lass." He seemed sincere as he left her alone to her food. She didn't even care that people were seemingly staring at her feast of one as she simultaneously ate from both plates.

As she finished up the last few bites she could manage, and ordered another lager to sip on, she fished her phone out of her bag once more. Still nothing from Callum. A few empty threats from Aiden. She texted Callum one last time and then made the resolve to not contact him again. If he couldn't even give her the benefit of the doubt and listen to her, then maybe she didn't love him like she thought she did, maybe he didn't care like he said he did.

As Charlotte was about to put her phone away, a voice call came through. She punched the accept button and held the phone to her ear.

"Hello…"

"Charlotte! It's Daisy! When are you home?" Charlotte smiled as soon as she realized her friend was calling. Somehow, Daisy always seemed to sense when Charlotte needed her. They'd been friends since grade school and now they both worked in education, though, granted, Daisy was an early education teacher while Charlotte was, well, struggling with a career she wanted.

"Oh Daisy. I'm so glad you called! I'll be home in a few days!"

"You sound low Char, what's going on?"

"Aiden came to see me in Edinburgh. He wants to bring me home."

"That would sound romantic if I didn't know what a control freak that man was. Seriously, why did you ever marry him again?"

"Honestly, I'm not sure. He was charming before he was ya know…"

"An abusive POS."

"Yeah…"

"Don't worry, you'll be home soon and can go back to ignoring his existence once you have that promotion."

"He says he's going to make sure I don't get it."

"Like he said he'd make sure you never worked, never got a car, never got a boyfriend?" Daisy was sarcastic, she was always sarcastic.

"This is different. This time he's actually friends with the Dean and could totally scupper my chances of promotion."

"Urgh, do you want to work for someone who is his friend?"

"I mean, he was charming before he wasn't, ya know?"

"Yeah, I guess so. Is anything else bothering you?"

"Um. Actually, yeah. I met someone while I was here…"

"OMG Char! Why didn't you start with that?!" Daisy's interruption made her laugh for the first time that day.

"Well... he kind of, thinks I'm married to Aiden."

"You didn't tell him you were divorcing?"

"I didn't get the chance to! He left when Aiden told him I was his wife!"

"Ah man, that sucks. Let me guess, now he's not answering your calls?"

"Exactly!"

"Give him space. If he's really that interested in, you then he'll hear you out once he gets his head around it. If he doesn't contact, you then he doesn't care enough." Daisy always had the right thing to say to make Charlotte feel better.

"Thanks Daisy! Call you tomorrow?"

"You'd better!"

Charlotte hung up the phone as the waiter came over with a box.

"What's that?" Charlotte was quizzical. She couldn't eat another mouthful without exploding.

"This my dear, is on me. It's a treat for the road."

"Thank you! You didn't have to do that, please, let me pay."

"Nah, I insist. You're too pretty to look so sad. Besides, soul food needs kindness to feed you, right?"

"Thank you", Charlotte laughed slightly as she took the box.

"Ah ah, wait til you get home to open it. It's a surprise."

Thanking him again, Charlotte left a big tip and made her way back to the hotel. All that good food and drink, her conversation with Daisy and that simple act of kindness had her spirits lifted.

....

14.

Walking across old stone bridges into the courtyard that housed the School of Business, Charlotte couldn't help but appreciate the stark contrast between the old masonry and the new, cutting edge corners of the Business building. Given what she'd already seen between the Old and New Towns of Edinburgh, she was pleasantly surprised to see a similar theme here at the University of Edinburgh.

Charlotte had arrived early, taking a taxicab, to make sure she got to her destination without getting lost. Despite the events of the night before with Callum and Aiden, she was still excited to meet with Dean Campbell to get first-hand experience of the software they'd created. She couldn't help but believe that if she really knew this software better than anyone else, with what she would learn here and what she'd already learned at the conference, then even Aiden couldn't ruin her chances of getting the promotion.

She spent a little more time exploring the area around the Business School, happy in her knowledge that she knew where to go when it was time to meet Dean Campbell. Part of her hoped that Callum would be in his offices, even though he had told her his office was in a different location because they worked in different departments, she still had a glimmer of hope. After all, him and Dean Campbell collaborated on software technology for fun, outside of either of their respective departments, so it was perfectly logical to assume she might get to see him, at least, that's what she had talked herself into when she dressed a little fancier than normal this morning.

"Charlotte, is that you?" Dean Campbell was hurting over to her in the quad.

"Oh yes, hello Dean Campbell. I was just looking around before our meeting."

"Ah please dear, call me Bernard. Come, we have much to discuss." Bernard led her into the Business School building. It was very modern looking, with floor to ceiling glass windowpanes lighting up the inside of the building, making everything look like summertime.

"What do you think of the campus my dear?"

"It's just as beautiful as the city! It's very peaceful here. I bet it's nice to work here, though I'm not sure you get much done with the views."

"Ah yes, it certainly is beautiful. Makes you want to stay, no?" Bernard chuckled a little as he peeked at her from behind long greying lashes.

"If only! I'm starting to really not want to leave this place. I've never felt quite so… serene."

"Scotland will do that to you. When are you due to go back to the States?"

"Three days' time. Maybe sooner."

"Oh? Eager to get back to that promotion, are you?"

"Maybe. I'm not sure if the promotion is even certain any more Dean… I mean, Bernard."

"This wouldn't have anything to do with Callum now would it?"

"Callum... did he tell you something?"

"No, no. He's been walking around like a bear with a sore head yesterday afternoon and this morning. First time I've seen him without a smile since you arrived."

"Oh." Charlotte didn't know what to make of the revelation. She just wished Callum would return her calls and messages.

"Ah well, these things have a way of working themselves out." His calm demeanor made Charlotte feel at ease.

....

Callum couldn't concentrate. He huffed out another breath as he went back to grading papers in his office. He didn't know if he was mad, angry, upset or disappointed. Mainly he felt sad. She was married?! They'd been so intimate, and he was sure she felt the same way he did.

He was sure she had feelings for him, and he knew now that what he was feeling for her was more than just a holiday fling. Or, what he had felt. He didn't know what to think now. How could she be married? And to him, Aiden, what an asshat! How could she have married someone like him?

Thoughts whirled through his head until he had to rub his temples to prevent a migraine. Callum thought back to their conversations before he'd met Aiden. She had mentioned him a couple of times. Heck, she'd had a damn nightmare about the man. Callum mentally kicked himself for leaving her in the cafe. What if she'd been in danger, hadn't she avoided answering about whether or not Aiden had been abusive to her? What was he thinking?

He should have remembered her feelings, but he was in too much shock to think much of anything except his own damn feelings. And now he'd lost her. She left for the States at the end of the week and he'd ignored about twenty messages from her. It was too late to call her now, no matter how he felt.

Callum went back to grading papers and tried to push thoughts of Charlotte out of his head. For once, those thoughts weren't of what he wanted to do to her, with her, but more what he wished he should have done back in that damn cafe.

....

"This is so cool!" Charlotte was excited to get the chance to handle the software in real time. The only time she'd had to use it before was with software demos that ended before anything exciting even happened.

"I'm glad you're enjoying it! You're a natural!" Bernard chuckled at Charlotte's excitement, clearly reveling in her enjoying the software he'd helped to create.

"Tell me dear, did you bring your resume like I asked?"

"Yes, here you go!" Charlotte pulled her resume out and handed it to Bernard. She was a little nervous for him to read it.

Bernard sat in silence for a long time while he perused Charlotte's resume. He was awed at some of the items on the list, and she'd done so well with her MBA grades. He wondered what had made her take the admin job but given she did it while she finished her degree, he'd bet it was more for ease of income than anything else. Not that there was anything wrong with that line of work, but with her experience, she could have taken on more responsibility.

The only thing missing from her resume was the promotion she was applying for. He'd like to ask her a bit more about it when the time was right. For now, he tucked her resume into his desk and went back to teach her more about his software. She was a natural.

....

Finishing up his final grading of papers, Callum sat back in his chair, contemplating what he should do about Charlotte.

Callum's office was large, though felt small because he shared the space with his colleague, Amelia. Piles and piles of papers were always stacked on each of their desks, though, granted, hers were always a little neater than his. Hers was littered with potted plants, while his just housed his computer and basic stationary. He wondered what Amelia would make of his predicament, he often shared his troubles with her, and vice versa.

As if my magic, Amelia busted through the door holding a new stack of papers.

"Urgh, why must there be so many pages!" She huffed as she dropped the pile onto her desk.

"Well, midterms are due my dear." Callum chuckled in spite of his current mood.

"Aye, next year I'm demanding everything come in through email." Amelia had a thick Scottish accent. She was from Glasgow originally but had come to Edinburgh to teach.

"Well then you'd be complaining about your full inbox."

"When's that software ready anyway?"

"We're working on it, lass."

Amelia was beautiful in her own way. She was short, with long blonde curls that fell about her shoulders. She was very blunt, and despite her beauty, she absolutely hated anyone pointing it out, or heaven forbid, calling her cute.

"How was class?"

"Same as usual at this time of year. Everyone is on edge; they're not really listening to what I have to teach them now unless I tell them it's in the final. Yours?"

"Same, same."

"You seem down, what's eating at you?" Amelia sat down at her desk, turning her chair to face Callum's desk.

....

Callum off loaded his troubles onto Amelie, and when he was done, she offered him her blunt and straightforward advice. Either he lives his life as it is, forgetting his romance and pretending it was simply a holiday flight, or he goes after Charlotte and enjoys the remainder of her stay.

Which path he should choose, Callum couldn't decide. Partly he was afraid that if he went after Charlotte, and she soon left to go back to Seattle, that he would want to go after her. Would it be better to just forget his feelings? Callum didn't know if he could even forget how he felt. Maybe that was his answer.

"Callum!" Amelie had been talking to him, but he was lost in his thoughts.

"Sorry, what were you saying?"

"The software? Will it be ready in time for finals?"

"I'm not sure. Bernard is working on the final platform release today. We need to make sure that the administration section works just as well as the grade input parts."

"Is there going to be a part for faculty to put notes in and stuff?"

"Yes, and messaging functionality."

"Alright, you need to make this happen for me, Callum. I can't spend much longer with my head buried in these damn papers."

"You best get back to it then!"

"Same goes for you! I see that pile behind you!"

....

15.

Although his work allowed some respite from his feelings, some slight distraction, he now had the space to think once again of Charlotte. He had to see her before she left, if nothing else but to clear the air. Amelie was right, he could either wallow in his feelings and shake the last few days off as a holiday romance, or he could fight for whatever it is that was between them.

The shrill sound of his office phone brought Callum back to reality. Answering it on the second ring, he found Bernard on the other end.

"Bernard, how can I help you?"

"Can you get over to the Business School? I could do with your eyes on a software bug." He sounded on edge, almost panicked, which was quite unlike Bernard.

"Absolutely, I'll be right there."

"Is Amelie with you?"

"Yes, why?"

"Bring her too. I could use another set of eyes on the faculty side."

"Alright, I'm sure she'd be happy to leave her grading!"

....

"Come on Amelie, I'm your knight in shining armor."

"How exactly?" Amelie answered without looking up from her stack of papers.

"Bernard needs you and me in his office."

"Me? Why me?"

"Something about needing your opinion on the faculty part of the software."

"Ooohoo nice. Let's go!"

On the short walk across campus to the Business building, Callum's mind raced. How could there be a bug in the software? Every time he'd used it or run updates, nothing had come up. He quickened his pace to get there faster. This was just the distraction he needed from Charlotte.

"Slow down, Callum. My legs aren't as long as yours!"

"Sorry, sorry!" Callum laughed and slowed his pace.

....

Callum knocked once and pushed open the door to Bernard's office.

"Bernard, we came as soon as we could….
Charlotte?" Callum couldn't believe it. What was she doing here?

"Callum…" his name came out on a whisper, he barely heard it.

"Callum, Amelie, come quick." Callum turned his eyes slowly away from Charlotte, frightened that if he looked away, she might disappear. Sensing the haste in Bernard's words, he tore his gaze away and rushed over to his side.

"Look." Bernard was bent over his computer screen, frowning, and pointing to the screen.

"How could it be? Here, move aside." Callum frowned as he tapped away at the computer.

Amelie stood watching Callum and Bernard work on the computer. She looked up and saw Charlotte eyeing her up and down.

"May I…?" Charlotte stepped next to Callum, gently taking the lead on the computer.

She typed away, not looking away from the screen, barely blinking and she calmly took the lead.

"Bernard, I checked this last night and nothing popped up. How did you find the bug?" Callum looked over at Bernard.

"Actually, Charlotte here was playing with the software so she might learn it better, and well, spotted the bug."

"You know how to do that?" Callum turned to Charlotte.

"Mmmhmm. I took a few computer classes to pick up a minor while I finished my MBA. I found it really more of a hobby than anything, like solving a puzzle." She spoke excitedly but didn't break her concentration with the computer.

The two men glanced at each other and looked at Charlotte in awe. Callum wasn't sure what to say, he was still reeling from the day before and the betrayal he felt at finding out she was married. He should probably leave; except he didn't want to. He wanted to be here with her, to breathe in her familiar scent.

....

Charlotte couldn't believe it when Callum walked through the door. She knew he would be coming because of Bernard's reaction to the software bug she'd found, but she didn't expect him to come with a woman.

Charlotte peeked at the woman, Amelie, who had come in with Callum. Her Callum. Who was she? She was stunningly beautiful, petite and focused on Callum. Charlotte was being silly, jealous even. She had no claim to Callum even if the two were an item.

Charlotte focused on the task at hand, it was a relatively easy fix, she'd seen things like it before. Though easy, it would still take a long time, time that she would have to spend with Callum. She was thankful Bernard was here to bridge the gap between them.

"Ok, I think I've got it." Charlotte was tired, having been working on the bug for hours.

"Marvelous!" Bernard came over to the computer screen to check the software.

"I built a firewall into the software, that way if another bug comes through, it should get caught before it causes any damage. I don't know the software code so you might want to check it and make sure nothing else was damaged."

Both men sat to take a look through the software. Amelie walked over to Charlotte and introduced herself.

"Are you close with Callum?" Charlotte couldn't help the question coming out, besides, she was genuinely curious.

"Sort of. We share an office." Amelie chuckled.

"Ah, ok. So, you teach literature, too?"

"I do, yes. I don't really have much to do with the software, but Bernard wanted my faculty opinion and Callum and I were already together when he called."

Charlotte wondered why they would be together. They seemed close, flirty even, when they spoke, but of course, if they shared an office, it was likely that's where they'd come from. Charlotte was being silly, jealous even, and that wasn't like her.

....

"Here, let me pull it up on my laptop." Callum had already started booting up his heavy looking laptop.

"Callum wrote the original code, my dear." Bernard's voice broke Charlotte's thoughts, clearly misreading her confused expression as wanting to know why Callum was pulling out his laptop.

Bernard looked eagerly at Callum as he worked. Charlotte wasn't sure what to do with herself, so she watched too. Callum didn't seem to notice his audience as he typed away, his entire concentration on his laptop. Amelie was also looking at Callum, smiling slightly as the men worked.

"Well, is it intact?" The worry in Bernard's voice had returned.

"Uh, yes. Yes, everything is there. I'll let the computer run some diagnostics overnight and double check, but I think it's fine."

"Phew!" Relief flooded Bernard's face as he paced over to his desk.

"This calls for a celebration!" Bernard produced a crystal bottle of whiskey and three glasses and handed them each one.

"Charlotte, we cannot thank you enough for spotting that dreadful bug." Bernard filled each of their glasses with a tot.

The three drank together in silence. Bernard looked from Callum to Charlotte and back again. Neither Charlotte of Callum could look at one another.

"I'm not sure what happened between the two of you, but you should sort it out before you regret it." Bernard was blunt.

"Amelie, can you look over the faculty piece for me?"

"Sure, let me see."

Amelie and Bernard leant close together as they worked. Charlotte wondered if there was something going on with them, but then she remembered he was married. Surely, he wouldn't get involved with someone behind Aileen's back.

"It's not what you think." Callum must have read her mind.

"Oh?"

"They're related. Amelie is the daughter of Bernard's cousin."

"Ah, I see. They seem close."

"They are. Bernard helped to raise her after she lost her parents."

Charlotte felt guilty for thinking something else was going on. Clearly her own experiences with men was shadowing her current experiences. Bernard was obviously a great man, her impression of him was even higher since Callum's admission about his kindness to his relative.

....

As Bernard and Amelie talked, Charlotte started to feel self-conscious, standing there alone, just feet away from Callum. She was starting to feel things for him that she didn't want to admit to herself, at least not yet. She was hyper aware that she would be leaving for Seattle soon and didn't know whether or not to let their romance die as a holiday romance, or whether it was the start of something bigger.

After what happened with Aiden, she didn't want to think about what might happen if she let herself have a chance with Callum. Still, she wasn't sure what Callum even wanted. He still hadn't returned any of her calls or messages.

"Charlotte... Can we talk?"

....

16.

It was late by the time Charlotte left Bernard's office. She had stayed to make sure she wasn't needed and that no more bugs or coding issues came to light. Not that she would be much help with coding, but if a bug came up in another part of the software, she could at least be useful in fixing that. Luckily, nothing had come up and the firewall she built would be able to at least warn them if an intruder attempt occurred again.

"Charlotte..." Callum called out to her as she stepped into the cool air.

"Callum. What's up?"

"What's up? That's what you're going with."

"I'm not sure what you want me to say."

"Can we talk?"

"Uh... sure, yes."

"Ok, how about over a drink? I have a feeling this conversation will need a little alcohol buffer."

Charlotte nodded her agreement, and since she didn't know that her voice would work over the nerves building in her stomach, she was glad her body was able to complete the movement.

Callum called a taxicab to take them into the city center. As they climbed out of the car, Charlotte felt chilled and anxious. She wasn't sure she was ready to share all of her secrets about Aiden but feared she would lose him if she didn't.

"Come, let's go in here." Callum led her into the closest bar.

Despite herself, Charlotte couldn't help but smile at the inside of the bar. Soft red chairs were scattered around small tables, and a giant hearth fireplace lined one wall. The bar wrapped around the other side of the building. Inside, people were chatting away lively, some engaged in deep conversations, others sitting staring into the fireplace as a large fire roared inside. It was peaceful and alive all at the same time, and made Charlotte feel like she was at home.

"Whiskey?" Callum appeared next to her, handing her a glass of liquid.

"Thank you."

He sat down next to the fireplace and motioned for Charlotte to sit next to him.

"So…" Callum spoke, but neither one of them seemed to know what to say. They both took a sip of their drinks.

"I've missed you, Charlotte."

"I've missed you, too."

"Tell me. Is that man really your husband?"

"Yes, no, technically yes." Charlotte's words were falling over one another.

"He... We used to be married. Technically we still are, the divorce hasn't been finalized yet, but it's a matter of time. Everything has been done, we're just waiting for the paperwork to go through."

"Why didn't you tell me?"

"I'm not sure. I didn't think it was relevant. I'm going home in a few days and I sure as heck didn't think Aiden would follow me to Scotland!"

"Yeah, I guess that makes sense. Just a few days, huh?"

"Yes. My flight leaves three days from now." Charlotte was sad when she said it aloud. She really didn't want to leave.

"I don't want you to go." Callum seemed sad himself.

"Truth be told, neither do I. Once Bernard started me thinking that staying was a possibility, I've been kind of sad, that I have to go home to Seattle."

"Thank you for today, for saving the software." Callum nodded.

"Oh, you're welcome, it was nothing really."

"That bug could have destroyed the entire software!"

"I suppose so yes." Charlotte laughed lightly.

"Oh, how I've missed that sound." Callum laughed gently, making Charlotte blush.

"Tell me, Charlotte, how did someone like you end up with someone like Aiden?"

"It's a long story."

"I'd like to hear it, if you want to tell me."

"Ok. It was not long after my parents had moved away and I was in Seattle, alone, with no real sense of direction. I had my job at the University, but it wasn't a career for me, it was just a job to pay the bills."

"I understand, and Aiden?"

"He worked above me, one of the senior managers. We became friends and he sort of pushed me to apply for the MBA. We had a bond, but he was sweet then."

"And he changed?"

"He did, but not until we were already married. I had started my MBA just after we got married. It wasn't anything big, just a quickie marriage, heck, my family didn't even get to attend."

"Why? A woman like you should have had a fairytale wedding."

"Haha, I don't know about that! Well, Aiden said he couldn't wait, so we just got married on a whim. It wasn't until I'd finished a few semesters of the MBA that he started to turn... mean."

"Mean? Mean, how?"

"I came home really happy one day, I'd just got my midterms back and it was looking like I would make straight A's, and I'd been asked to apply for a fellowship! I remember being so excited. When I got home, Aiden was upset with me, he thought I was happy because I'd been cheating. When I told him, it was because of my grades, he lost it. Called me lots of names and eventually struck me."

Charlotte was speaking so fast; she wasn't sure that Callum could keep up. She looked up at him and noticed the muscle of his jaw flexing and unflexing, almost like he wanted to say something but daren't.

"Go on…" Callum seemed to strain the words out of his mouth. His fists clenched in his lap.

"Well, once he'd struck me once, he would strike me whenever he felt the need to. Usually it would be on the legs, or in places that wouldn't show at work. He liked to pinch me too."

"What made you finally leave him?"

Charlotte tensed up and brought her knees to her chest. She trembled slightly as she picked up her whiskey glass.

"It's ok, you don't have to tell me. Charlotte, let me take you home."

She nodded and a single tear dripped onto her cheek. Callum reached for her hand and led her to the door.

....

Charlotte opened the door to her hotel room and let Callum in behind her. She kicked off her shoes and sat on the edge of the bed. Callum sat next to her.

"I should go." Callum started to rise from the bed.

"No, please don't." Charlotte reached out to stop him from leaving.

"Ok. You don't have to tell the rest of the Aiden story; we can talk about something else."

"No, I want to. I want to tell you." Charlotte turned to Callum and he nodded, waiting for her to resume the story.

"One night, I was working late at the University. There was a huge issue with a piece of software we were using for data input and because I'd been taking extra classes with my MBA, I stayed to help with it. It ended up being just me and a coworker, Jack, working quite late. I don't remember what time it was, but it had definitely got dark outside. We were about to finish up and go home when Aiden came bursting through the door. He'd been drinking quite heavily by the smell of him and was furious. I'd called and told him why I was working late, but I guess he didn't believe me."

"Did he hit you, in front of your coworker?"

"Oh yes, and he didn't stop. Jack had tried to pull him off, but Aiden was much stronger than him and pushed him to the floor. Jack ran off to get help...." Tears were running down Charlotte's cheeks at the memory.

"Jesus, Charlotte. What happened?" Callum looked pained as he spoke, like he was trying to restrain himself.

"I ended up in the hospital. He'd broken two of my ribs, my eye socket and split my lip pretty badly. I was there for about a week, I think. I just remember being pretty groggy. My friend Daisy came to get me, and I moved in with her."

"Why is this pig still working for the University? Why isn't he in jail?!"

"His uncle works in upper administration at the University. He promised them that he would stay away from me and enter into a special program for anger management so that he could keep his job."

"And did he? Stay away from you I mean?"

"Of course not. I had to threaten a restraining order, but he basically followed me everywhere I went, sent threatening messages."

"How long did this go on for?"

"I'm not sure, maybe a year. Eventually he got bored, but he still kept tabs on me. I didn't dare date or do anything that I knew would make him mad."

"And now he's here, why?"

"He didn't like me taking vacation, I guess. He's threatened my promotion chances if I don't go back with him."

"He doesn't have that power, surely."

"Sort of. His best friend is the Dean in charge of the promotion, and like I said, he's related to upper administration, so no-one wants to cross him. Everyone knows he has a temper."

"Christ, Charlotte. I'm so sorry. I wish I'd known sooner. I could have protected you from him."

Callum reached out to take her hand. She looked up at him and smiled through tear-soaked lashes. Charlotte sniffed and looked down at her lap, where their conjoined hands laid. His hand was so big compared to hers, so safe.

"Callum…?"

"Yes?"

"Will you please stay with me tonight and just… hold me?"

"I'd love to, if you'll have me."

"Yes, please."

"I should never have left that cafe. I should have listened to you, I'm so sorry, Charlotte."

"It's ok. You thought I'd lied to you or betrayed you. I get it."

The pair got ready for bed quickly. Callum held her tightly until she fell soundly asleep. He needed her to feel the love he had for her through his arms as he held her.

....

17.

"So, you have a few days left. What do you want to do with your time? Name it and I'll make it happen." Callum was still holding Charlotte as they woke up. He had made a promise to himself to make Charlotte's last few days in Scotland the best of her life.

"Mmm... I'm not sure. This... This would be good." Callum was lightly stroking her arms and neck as she spoke, making her lose track of her thoughts.

"We can't just stay in bed and waste the last few days you have." Callum smiled, amused at her response.

"Sure, we can. I would like that very much."
Charlotte turned to face him in the bed and kissed him
gently.

Callum kissed her back, long and gentle. She returned
his kiss, increasing the urgency as she climbed on top
of him.

"Are you sure you want to do this?" Callum was
breathless when he spoke.

"Absolutely…" She kissed him again and ground her
hips against his, bringing a groan from his lips.

"Charlotte…" Her name came out on a groan.

His erection pressed into her hips, making her smile
lazily. She slowly rubbed her center across his
clothed erection as she kissed him deeply. He reached
around to cup her bottom, trailing his fingers along
the line of the fabric of her panties. She arched her
back as he slipped a finger beneath the hem and found
her center.

"You're ready for me…" he whispered against her.

His fingers pushed inside her, and she bucked against
them, deepening his intimate touch. She rocked
against him, his fingers making love to her as she
groaned against the pleasure ripping through her. She
increased the speed of her rocking until she felt her
orgasm building.

"Callum… I'm going to…"

"Come for me, Charlotte. I've got you."

She came at his demand and he gently removed his fingers, pulling her against him. His erection strained against his shorts. Charlotte stood and threw her clothes off. Callum quickly yanked his own clothes onto the pile on the floor and pushed himself to the end of the bed. Charlotte stood, naked, between his legs.

"You're so beautiful, Charlotte. We have some time to make up for."

"Mmm, we sure do."

"Turn around."

Callum palmed Charlotte's backside and lifted her onto his erection. He groaned at the feel of her against his penis, she was so warm and wet, ready for him. Charlotte moved against him until he couldn't take any more and came hard.

....

Sometime later, Callum and Charlotte lay naked together in the bed. They were on top of the covers, their bodies were entwined with one another, sated from their lovemaking.

"I think that definitely made up for the time we lost." Charlotte laughed at Callum's joke.

"Yes, I'd sure say so!"

"Let's get some food, I'm starving."

"I don't want to get dressed. Can we order to the room?"

"Sure, anything you want in particular?"

"Surprise me." Charlotte was sleepy as she spoke.

Callum got up and without getting dressed, he called down to room service. Charlotte rolled over and lazily closed her eyes as she stretched her naked body against the warm fabric of the bed sheets.

By the time room service knocked at the door, Charlotte had fallen into a deep sleep. The sound of Callum opening the door roused her. That's odd, she thought. The sounds she heard didn't sound cordial at all, more like people arguing. She sat up in bed, using the bed sheet to cover up her naked body, sparks of fear shooting up her spine.

Charlotte heard scuffling coming from the door of the hotel room, but before she could get up to see what was going on, Callum came hurting past the bed, landing solidly on the floor. Before she could blink, Aiden came crashing down on top of Callum, landing punch after punch. Charlotte screamed.

"Aiden! Get off him! What are you doing?!"

"She's MY wife, how dare you sleep with MY wife!" Aiden was red with rage, pummeling Callum.

Charlotte leapt off the bed, wrapping the sheet tight around her as she went to help Callum.

"I said get off him!" Aiden turned on Charlotte, knocking her out cold.

When Charlotte came to, she couldn't move from the floor. She tried to open her eyes, but one wouldn't open at all. With her one good eye, she saw Callum slowly getting off the floor and charging at Aiden. The two scuffled, throwing each other into the walls, furniture, and finally onto the floor, before getting back up and throwing more punches at each other.

Charlotte wasn't sure how much time had passed with the two fighting, when Aiden landed a blow to Callum's head that had him stumbling backwards. Callum lost his balance and landed square on the floor, Charlotte tried to scream but her voice failed her.

She closed her eyes for a second, and when they opened, she saw Aiden's feet coming towards her. He yanked her up and threw her on the bed.

"Get dressed." He spat the words at her and turned his attention to Callum.

Charlotte stood on unsteady legs and hurried to the bathroom as fast as she could. The blow to her face had left her disoriented. She looked over at Callum as she made her way out of the room, she could see that he was breathing, but he was out cold. Blood covered his face, making her think his nose had been broken, or worse.

She stood looking at herself in the bathroom mirror, inspecting the damage of her eye. Her left eye was closed shut, bruising was already starting to show around the edges and up to her eyebrow. There wasn't any blood, thankfully, and nothing else seemed off. Given her last violent encounter with Aiden had left her in the hospital, she was feeling pretty thankful the damage wasn't much worse. But Callum, the thought of Callum lying there made her stomachache.

"What's taking so long?!" Aiden sounded furious.

She quickly got dressed and came out of the bathroom to face him. Callum was still lying on the floor, though this time he was groaning. She willed him to stay down without saying a word.

"Pack your things, we're leaving."

"Where are we going?" Her voice was timid, but she wanted to scream.

"Home. I'm taking you back to Seattle where you can't whore yourself out."

Charlotte started packing up her suitcase with whatever she could find on the floor. While Callum and Aiden were yelling at each other, she spotted her passport lying on the floor and gently placed it under Callum's phone on the nightstand. If Aiden was going to take her to the airport, neither of them would get far if she didn't have her passport.

"She's going nowhere with you, pal." Callum stood up shakily and squared his shoulders at Aiden.

"Says who? Pretty bad fighter for a Scotsman aren't ya?"

Callum swung at Aiden again, this time connecting solidly in his nose. Blood splattered where Aiden's nose broke on impact, leaving him grunting. Aiden sat on the bed as Callum reached for Charlotte.

"Charlotte, let's go." Callum's voice was calm considering the fight. Charlotte stood rooted in place.

"If you go with him, I'll find you soon enough Charlotte. You can't escape me and if you care for him, if you want him to live, you'll go back to Seattle with me." Aiden's words were harsh, and Charlotte knew from experience he was serious.

"I'm sorry Callum, but he's right. I have to stay with him."

"What?!" It was Callum's turn to look furious. "You can't stay with him!"

"I have to, to protect you. I've seen what he can do."

Aiden's smug grin made Callum want to smack him another time. Charlotte looked downcast and heartbroken; she was shivering where she stood.

"Go on loverboy, leave." Aiden spat at Callum.

"At least let me say goodbye." Charlotte asked softly.

Aiden nodded in disgust, turning his back to Charlotte and Callum. Charlotte slowly and quietly walked up to Callum, she put her arms around him and reached up on tiptoes to whisper into his ear.

"When we've gone, call the police. It's the only way. I love you Callum."

Callum stood in shock, he felt dumbfounded that she would risk her life like this, just for him, for them. He watched Aiden smugly push Charlotte through the door, desperately wanting to finish the fight and put him down for good, but he had to do what Charlotte had told him to.

As soon as Aiden and Charlotte had closed the door, Callum called the police and told them the situation. He hoped to God they got there in time to stop Aiden from taking the love of his life from him. He hadn't even had the chance to tell her he loved her too.

....

18.

By the time the police arrived at the hotel, Aiden and Charlotte were long gone. Callum could have cried with frustration that he'd even let them leave. He was sitting on the bed in the hotel room, which was almost covered in blood. The police were questioning him about what had happened and who Aiden was.

Callum told them all he knew. That Aiden was taking her home to Seattle, about his violent history with her and about what had happened in the hotel room. He was starting to panic with the amount of time that was passing with Charlotte in Aiden's clutches. God knows what he would do with her between the time it took to get from the hotel to the airport.

The policeman spoke on his radio phone with someone Callum presumed to be his colleague. They were relaying his description of Charlotte and Aiden to someone on the other end of the radio, telling them to get to the airport and detain them. Callum hoped it wasn't too late.

As the two policemen spoke to one another about heading to the airport, Callum looked around the room to see if he could find his cell phone. Settling on the nightstand, he saw something sitting underneath his phone. He reached over and picked up his phone and noticed the passport sitting underneath, flipping it open, he realized it was Charlotte's passport! She must have left it for him when he scuffled with Aiden!

"Officers! She left her passport for us!"

"That's great news, at least we know she can't leave the country. Let's head to the airport."

Callum got up to come with them.

"Sir, it's probably best if you stay here."

"No chance! She put herself in danger to save my life, I'm coming!"

"Alright, just promise us when this is over you get checked out at the hospital and stay back when we engage."

"Yes, I promise, let's go!"

....

Charlotte was shaking when Aiden almost threw her into his car. He must have got a rental to avoid having to take a taxicab to the airport. The throbbing of her eye kept her preoccupied and she tried to stop the fear from taking control of her body.

She wanted to run, to scream, to do something to get out of the car with him. She didn't dare look at him, rather, she could sense his anger and disgust. Peeking out of the corner of her eye, she saw Aiden's grip tightening on the steering wheel, steely eyes focused sharply on the road in front of him, his normally pale skin was red with anger, and his features were scrunched up with rage.

"Why do you hate me so much, Aiden?" The words slipped out of her mouth before she could stop them. He turned to her and she flinched.

"Charlotte, I love you. More than that, I am obsessed with you. I can't not have you." His words were scary as they fell out of his upturned mouth.

"But it's been over for a long time. We aren't together anymore. We will never be together, Aiden." She spoke softly, but her words were strong.

"If I can just get you back to Seattle, you'll see."

"No. Even when I go back to Seattle, I won't be with you. We don't belong together."

"I'll get help, Charlotte. I'll go back to anger management classes, anything to be with you."

"Aiden, you're not hearing me. Hear me when I say, we will never be together. Not here, not in Seattle, not anywhere. I don't love you."

Charlotte stopped talking when she saw Aiden grip the steering wheel so hard that his knuckles turned white. She'd angered him again, but she didn't care anymore. She needed to be strong and let him know that there was no way back to her.

"Aiden. I cared for you once, that much is true. You need help. If you don't get your anger checked, you'll end up killing someone, or worse. I want you to get help."

Aiden and Charlotte drove the rest of the way to the airport in silence. Charlotte only hoped that Callum had done what she'd told him to do and called the police. He should have found her passport by now, that would slow her and Aiden down once they got to the airport. She hoped Callum was ok, she didn't dare think about the damage Aiden had done to him with all those punches. She knew from firsthand just how painful it was to recover from a beating like that from Aiden.

As Aiden drove, Charlotte wondered what had happened to make him the way he was. Why was he so angry and hate filled? She knew it was nothing she had done, heck, she knew well enough to know it was nothing to do with her at all. His rage might be directed at her, and now Callum, but the reason behind it was nothing to do with her, with Seattle, with Callum or with Edinburgh.

....

Callum arrived at the airport not long after the police. He was shaking with nerves, his thoughts erratic as he worried whether or not Charlotte and Aiden had made it to the airport. He hoped she was safe, she had to be. The airport was small, the police should be able to find them fairly quickly, especially because he held Charlotte's passport in his hand.

He looked up and down the length of the airport, at least as far as he could go without a ticket or booking. He couldn't see Charlotte or Aiden anywhere. Several police officers stood at several points within the airport, talking into their walkie talkies, but still he didn't see Charlotte or Aiden. Where were they?

....

As they arrived at the airport, Charlotte turned to Aiden, laying her hand over his to stop him from getting out of the car.

"Please don't do this, Aiden. Not like this."

"Get out of the car, Charlotte, we have a plane to catch."

Charlotte stepped out of the car, worrying how Aiden would react when he realized she didn't have her passport. Hopefully, Callum would have brought the police to the airport, or at least alerted them, before they got that far.

"Here, put these on." Aiden handed her some dark sunglasses to hide her swollen eye. Though she could open it more now than she could in the hotel room, the bruising was still starting to come out, still, she slid the glasses in place.

Aiden and Charlotte stepped into the airport and a chill came up her spine. She felt like she was being watched. Looking around the entrance to the airport, Charlotte saw numerous police officers dotted around. She wondered if they were always there or if they were here for her. She studied the people in the airport, looking for Callum, or for anyone that she knew. Of course, she only knew a handful of people in Edinburgh, but she was hopeful that there would be someone who could help her.

"Sir? Sir? Excuse me, stop please." The stern sound made Charlotte stop and turn around. She felt Aiden tense next to her.

Aiden stopped and turned to come face to face with a police officer.

"Can I help you, officer?"

"What's your name pal?"

"Aiden… Aiden Smith, why?"

"And you miss, what's your name?" Charlotte turned to the policeman.

"Charlotte Wilson."

"What's this about?" Aiden's voice seemed irritated, annoyed.

"I need you both to come with me, please."

"I said, what is this about?" Aiden was growing impatient.

Two more police officers joined the first, ready to take Aiden into custody. Charlotte willed him to go willingly.

"We have a few questions for you, sir. Don't make me ask again."

Surprisingly, Aiden went with the policemen without another word, clearly wanting to get their questioning over so they could be on their way back to Seattle.

"Miss, please come with me." A female officer escorted Charlotte to a separate room, while Aiden was taken somewhere else.

"Miss, can you tell me what happened, please? We had reports about the man you were traveling with."

Charlotte told the officer everything that led to this point, including the history she shared with Aiden and what brought her to Edinburgh. She was tired and hungry; her eye was aching as much as her heart was. She wanted to go home but didn't quite know where home was.

"Ma'am, is there a Callum here?"

"Yes! We had him wait out of sight. You can see him when we finish up your statement."

Charlotte continued to answer questions, choosing to go ahead and press charges for assault in the hopes that it would allow Aiden to get the help he needed. He needed to take responsibility for his actions before he could get help for his anger.

"What will happen to him, to Aiden?" Despite the pain and anger she felt, she was also worried.

"He will be taken back to the United States and dealt with there. We're working with the U.S. Marshalls, and because most of this history stems from your history over there, it's best he's dealt with there."

Charlotte felt sick to her stomach, she didn't want any of this, but knew it was best.

....

"Callum!" Charlotte shouted after him as she exited the interview room. He turned around at the sound of her voice and came to her. He was walking slowly, pained.

Finally, the gap between them was closed and they embraced. Callum groaned in pain as she clung to him. She pulled away and looked up at him.

"Are you alright?"

"I'm fine, the paramedics gave me a once over. My ribs are bruised is all. I'll survive."

"Oh Callum, I'm so sorry! Is there anything I can do?"

"Some TLC would heal me pretty quickly I should think, and maybe some food. I'm starving."

"Me too! Let's get some food first."

"What about you, are you ok?" Callum embraced Charlotte as he asked about her.

"I'll be ok. I need to call my job back home and let them know what happened."

"Let's get food first, then job."
Callum led Charlotte out of the airport and to his car. They walked slowly, both exhausted and hurting.

....

19.

Just as Charlotte and Callum were about to climb into his car, they heard footsteps running towards them. They were fast and heavy in the dark parking garage. Charlotte whirled around just in time to see Aiden charging at her from across the lot. How had he escaped from the airport police?

Callum heard the footsteps at the same time as Charlotte, he turned to see her expression before he caught sight of Aiden running at full pelt towards them. He didn't look like he was going to stop. Callum thought Aiden was going to run straight through Charlotte.

Despite the pain in his ribs, Callum charged Aiden before he could reach Charlotte. He felt rage build inside him. With one punch, Callum knocked Aiden to the ground. He called for Charlotte to get the police. Before she could move, the police were already heading towards them, tasers drawn and focused on Aiden.

Aiden lay on the floor, knocked out from Callum's single punch.

"We're not doing this again, buddy." Callum held his ribs, clearly in pain, as he spoke quietly to Aiden.

Charlotte watched as two police officers dragged Aiden to fit feet, pulling him along, back to the airport.

"Come on, let's get that food."

Charlotte didn't feel much like eating inside a restaurant, instead she wanted to curl up to Callum and try to forget the horror that they had just been through.

Callum must've felt the same way as he pulled into Edinburgh city center and parked up.

"Stay here, lock the door after me. I'll go and grab us some food. We can eat at home."

"Home?" Charlotte wondered where that even was. She'd never seen Callum's apartment.

"I figured you wouldn't want to go back to the hotel. You can stay with me for your last few days."

Callum climbed out the car, grimacing with the pain in his ribs. Charlotte locked the door and looked around. She knew that Callum would be on his way back to Seattle now with a police escort, but she still felt on edge.

She didn't have to wait long before Callum came back to the car with two plastic bags with a Chinese shop label on them. She pressed the button to unlock the car door and he quickly slid in, handing the packages to her.

"Oh my god, this smells amazing." She inhaled deeply. The smell of warm Chinese food filled the car. It smelled sweet and hot all at the same time. Her mouth started to fill with water at the anticipation of the feast, and her stomach growled audibly, making Callum laugh.

"Me too, me too." He gently patted her stomach and laughed.

Putting the car into gear, Callum pulled off, heading toward his apartment in the city. Charlotte couldn't wait to see where he lived. She was a bit surprised that they hadn't been there yet, but her hotel seemed closer to where they had visited.

....

Callum pulled into his building parking lot and helped Charlotte out of the car. She was awed by the beauty of his apartment. The old stone masonry took Charlotte's breath away, the whole building gave the appearance of a Dickens novel.

As he unlocked the door and they stepped inside, she was awed to see the inside was almost as beautiful as the outside, and nothing that she would have imagined from a single man living by himself.

"Go ahead and look around while I get the food ready." Callum smiled at her.

Charlotte reveled in getting to look around houses. Even back at home, she would often look on real estate websites just so she could peek at other people's decor or apartment layouts.

The living room had a beautiful fireplace and two floor-to-ceiling windows that overlooked the city. The entire apartment had antique hardwood floors that gave everywhere a cozy feeling. Callum had rugs in every room that gave a warm feeling against the hard floors. Despite the basic furniture he had, the whole apartment felt really cozy and safe. She almost felt like she was at home.

Making her way back to the living room and kitchen area, Charlotte saw that Callum had already piled the Chinese food on two plates and poured two glasses of white wine. She sat down at the dining table facing him and felt relaxation spread over her for the first time since they'd been alone that morning.

Just as she was about to tuck into the food, her phone rang. Looking down at the caller ID, she noticed it was a Seattle area code.

"I'm sorry, this is back home. I just have to take this."

Charlotte stood up and answered the phone, pacing across the living room floor as she did so.

"Hello…"

"Charlotte? Is that you?"

"It's me. Who's this?"

"It's Dean Cooper, do you have a minute to talk? I'm not sure what time it is with you."

"Sure. What's up?" It was quite unusual for him to be calling her personal phone, and even more so while she was on vacation.

"Listen. I heard what happened with Aiden. Are you alright?"

"Oh, yes. I'm ok. Thank you. It's sweet of you to call and ask how I am."

"Actually, that's not the only reason I'm calling. I have some bad news I'm afraid."

"Oh?"

"Yes, I'm afraid I got a call from someone higher up not long ago. They're cancelling the software implementation, which means the job that goes with it is no longer viable."

"Oh no! So, no promotion? Why? How could this happen?" Charlotte's sadness came rushing back to replace the relaxed feeling she just had.

"That's right. There won't be a promotion anymore and we didn't really get an understanding of why. Maybe budget cuts? The upper administration just told me that we will no longer be able to host the software or the position that goes with it."

"Oh. What about my admin job?" Disappointment and fear for the future filled her voice.

"Don't worry about that, you'll always have your admin job."

"Ok, thank you."

"See you next week?"

"Yes, next week. Bye."

Charlotte hung up the phone and let the tears run freely down her face. The only reason she'd come here was because of the promotion. First, they'd made her fight for it and now they'd just taken it away, with no real reason as to why! Just a 'higher up' cancelled the program! Charlotte knew this had something to do with Aiden, after all, he was related to the 'higher ups'! If anyone could stop her getting the promotion, it was him.

"Is everything ok, Charlotte?" Callum came up behind her, putting his hands around her waist.

"They cancelled my promotion." Tears streamed from her eyes as Callum took her into a bear hug.

"I'm so sorry, Charlotte. What can I do?"

"Just hold me." Charlotte felt so sad and defeated. What would she do now? Go back to Seattle for her admin job and back to square one? She didn't want that!

"Come, let's eat."

....

Charlotte didn't want to eat, but she knew she had to, she'd barely eaten anything all day and felt sick to her stomach. She ate slowly, thinking about what she was going to do. Callum stole glances at her from behind his own food. He didn't seem to eat much either. Mainly they both sipped the wine until Charlotte became vaguely aware of Callum getting up to grab another bottle from the fridge.

"Come, sit with me." Refilling her wine glass, Callum handed it to her as he stood and led her to the sofa.

"You're shivering." She wasn't sure if she was actually cold, or if it was the events of the day that had her cold to the bone, but she was thankful for Callum getting up to put the fireplace on.

It had started to get dark as they sat together, silently watching the flames flicker in the fireplace. The only light came from a single spotlight above the dinner table in the corner of the kitchen, and the streetlights coming through the window below. The fireplace gave an eerie glow to the rest of the room, one that Charlotte felt oddly comforting.

Callum put his arm around Charlotte and pulled her close to his as they nestled together on the sofa. He wanted to erase the pain of the day, to take Charlotte's pain away, but he didn't know how. He wished she could stay with him and wondered if that might be an option now her promotion had been scuppered. It didn't take a genius to work out who was behind it, clearly Aiden had been able to access a phone from wherever he was. He hugged her tighter and felt her relax under his warmth.

After a while, Callum noticed Charlotte's breathing change. She'd fallen asleep against him. He put his wine glass on the side table next to him and gently picked her up. As he stood with her, his ribs burned under his sweater, but he pushed through the pain to carry her to his bed. Gently removing her boots and socks, he covered her up and settled her into the bed.

Deciding to take the spare bedroom so she had some space, he gently kissed her on the forehead before closing the door.

As Callum cleaned up the kitchen and turned off the fireplace, an idea popped into his head. What if she didn't have to go home? What if she could work at the University here, with him? He quickly checked on Charlotte to make sure she was still sleeping and pulled out his phone.

....

20.

"Callum! I wondered when you'd finally call!" Dean Campbell didn't seem at all surprised to hear from him.

"Bernard… You knew I would be calling about this?"

"I had hoped actually. Ever since I saw her resume, I had wanted to find a place for her here, but I didn't want to overstep my bounds if it wasn't something, she would be interested in. Plus, Amelie had a word in my ear about it all."

"Amelie, of course! I think she might be, at least I hope she might be interested!"

"She was quite something when she found the bug in our software. Do you think she would consider my offer?"

"I hope so! Do you want me to do the groundwork?"

"No, no. I'll call and arrange for her to visit. How long does she have left until she has to leave for Seattle?"

"Just a day. She leaves after tomorrow."

"Alright, I'll call her first thing in the morning."

....

Charlotte was awakened by the sound of whispering coming from the kitchen. She checked her watch, it was late. Who would Callum be talking to this late at night? She heard Amelie's name come from Callum's lips and she gasped.

So, it was Amelie? Is that who he was whispering to so late? Charlotte suspected there was something between them, they would always flirt openly. Callum had told her before that he saw her as a sister, but Charlotte wasn't so sure. Even coworkers she was close with wouldn't be whispering to her this late at night.

Charlotte made the decision there and then to go back to Seattle, back to her job and her friends. Her and Callum couldn't be together. What they had was clearly just a holiday romance, and now he was setting the stage with Amelie to continue his life with her once she left. At least, that's what his phone call had sounded like. No wonder he didn't stay in the bed with her, he'd already moved on!

She got back into the bed and set the alarm on her phone to leave his house early. He was close enough to the city for her to be able to jump in a taxicab, and she already had her bag here. She'd go straight to the airport and get her flight moved to a day earlier, there was nothing keeping her in Scotland now, especially now she didn't need to learn anything else about the software.

....

When Callum awoke, it was late. He'd slept in. The night before he'd lain in bed thinking about Charlotte and the real possibility that she might stay. He'd been nervous and excited all at once. He lay in the bed for a moment, smiling to himself as he imagined the life that he and Charlotte could have together in Scotland, both working for the University.

As he laid in the bed, he listened for sounds of Charlotte moving around, but heard only silence. He raised himself up on his elbows and listened more intently but heard nothing.

Panicking slightly, Callum rose from the bed and opened the door. He called her name but heard nothing. Slowly making his way to her room, he pushed open the door and found the room empty, the bed made neatly, and her things gone. He ran into the living room and again found it empty.

Callum wondered where she'd gone, and why she'd left without saying goodbye. Was she with Bernard? He knew Bernard would be calling her in the morning, and Callum had slept in. Maybe she'd not wanted to wake him and had gone to see Bernard at the University.

Flipping the kettle on to make coffee, Callum rested his forearms on the kitchen counter and laid his head in his hands. Looking up from his arms, his eyeline focused on the dining table and his phone sitting there, he went to it and punched in Bernard's number.

"Bernard…. Is Charlotte with you?"

"No, I thought she was staying with you?"

"Have you called her yet, about the job?"

"I tried to; I couldn't get through. I was just about to try again."

"Let me know if you hear from her?"

"Of course. Is something wrong?"

"Not yet, no. Talk to you soon!"

Callum hung up the phone and got dressed quickly. He grabbed his keys, wallet and phone and headed out the door. Coffee could wait.

....

Callum pulled into the hotel parking lot, barely putting the car into park before jumping out and heading for the front door. He hurried across the lobby and up to the front desk.

"Hi, did Charlotte Wilson check out today?"

"Let me check." The clerk typed quickly into the computer. Callum's nerves frayed with each touch of the keyboard.

"Ok, it looks like she checked out about an hour ago."

"Ok, thank you." Callum backed away from the reception desk, unsure of what his next move should be.

Callum stepped into his car and sat for a while without turning the ignition.

....

Charlotte made her way to the airport, deciding to take a taxicab instead of waiting on the airport shuttle. As she sat in the back seat, she observed the city as it passed her by. Edinburgh was a beautiful place, one in which she would have loved to stay in, but without Callum and without a job, she wasn't sure that was possible for her.

She wondered what had happened to Aiden, whether or not he was still in custody in Seattle. Daisy had called her as she packed up the rest of her things that had been left in the hotel room. She'd let Charlotte know that the Dean had fired Aiden, and despite Charlotte's promotion having been taken away, the Dean clearly saw fit to still remove Aiden from his post. At least when Charlotte returned to her admin post, she would be able to do so without fear or Aiden being in the next building or following her around campus. That was one piece of information that lifted her spirits as she got ready to head back to Seattle.

"We're here miss".

The taxi driver had pulled over and jumped out of the car to help with her bags before Charlotte had even understood what he'd said. She slowly stepped out into the cold, windy air and thanked the driver. Grabbing her suitcase and travel bag, she pulled her jacket closer to her and made her way into the airport.

....

"Bernard! Bernard…." Callum knocked on Bernard's office door. He'd tried to enter but it was locked.

"Callum, my dear boy, what can I do for you?"

Bernard came up behind Callum. He was carrying a laptop and a stack of books. Helping him unlock the office door, Callum wasn't sure exactly what he was asking Bernard for.

"Did you manage to get hold of Charlotte?"

"Ah no, I tried a few times earlier but didn't get a response, and then I had class." Bernard turned to face Callum, his eyebrows knitting together.

"Is everything alright, Callum?"

"Not really, Bernard. I think Charlotte has gone back to Seattle, and I'm not sure why she left without saying anything."

"Have you tried to call her?"

"Yes, and I went by her hotel to see if I could catch her. I can't get through to her phone, it keeps going to voicemail."

"Yes, that's the same issue I had. In the end I just left a message asking her to call me back."

"God damn, what shall I do?"

"You could always go to the airport and see if she's there. Heck, if you love her that much, you should just fly to Seattle and wait for her."

Bernard chuckled, but Callum had been considering it. He'd never ever had the chance to tell her how he felt about her.

"Let me call her one more time." Bernard called after him but Callum was already gone.

....

Charlotte sat at the gate in the airport with her luggage around her. She wasn't able to get a flight out for hours, but she didn't want to go back into the city, so had decided to wait it out in the airport. Picking up a trash magazine and some burnt tasting coffee, she sank into the uncomfortable chair and tried to relax. After a few minutes, she decided she would call Daisy and pass some time. Pulling out her phone, she realized her battery had died. She fished out the phone charger from her bag and plugged it into the adapter underneath her chair.

Waiting a few minutes for the charge to take, she turned on her phone. Messages and voicemail alerts bombarded her phone screen. She wasn't sure what to look at first! Scrolling through her messages, she saw a few from Callum, one from Daisy, one from Bernard and two from Aiden. She opened the ones from Callum first, and as she did so, her heart skipped a beat or two.

WHERE ARE YOU? WHY'D YOU LEAVE SO SOON? I NEED TO SEE YOU. I WANT TO TALK TO YOU, CHARLOTTE. PLEASE.

She then opened the messages from Aiden.

CHARLOTTE, I'M SO SORRY. FORGIVE ME? I LOST MY JOB AT THE UNIVERSITY. I'M NOT MAD. ENROLLING IN ANGER MANAGEMENT, MAYBE ONE DAY WE CAN BE FRIENDS?

The message from Daisy was just expressing excitement about her coming home to Seattle, suggesting they meet for coffee as soon as they could. Charlotte opened the message from Bernard.

TRIED TO CALL DEARIE. WANT TO TALK TO YOU BEFORE YOU GO HOME TOMORROW. PLEASE CALL BACK. BERNARD.

Charlotte wondered which to answer first. She tapped out a reply to Daisy, the easiest of the messages to respond to. She had no idea what to say to Callum, had she got it wrong? Was he not really involved with Amelie like she'd thought? Maybe she'd misunderstood the phone call she'd overheard from the night before. Even so, they couldn't be together, she had to go home eventually, there was no future for them together.

Deciding to first speak with Bernard, she tapped out a response to let him know her phone battery had died, that she was at the airport waiting for her flight home and asking what he wanted to speak to her about. Before she had a chance to respond to Callum, her phone was ringing. It was Bernard.

....

21.

"Charlotte, I'm so glad I caught you before you got on that dang plane."

"Bernard, is everything ok?" Charlotte was uncertain what he wanted, but he sounded relieved to have got her on the phone.

"Yes dear, quite fine. I wanted to speak with you about the University of Edinburgh and your plans for the future."

"Oh?"

"Tell me, did you enjoy your stay dear?"

"Yes, very much!"

"Would you consider staying?"

"Staying? Actually, yes. I have been thinking about staying from the minute I got here. I think I rather fell in love with the city. But I have a job back in Seattle. There isn't much for me here."

"What if I could offer you a job? A career? Perhaps the rest would come."

"A job?! That would be amazing, what kind of job?"

"With me. Working on software, fixing bugs, and managing a team to implement it across the University."

"But what about when the project is over?"

"People will always need training, there will always be software and there will always be fixes that need doing. It would be a permanent position."

"Oh wow. It sounds amazing! But, where would I stay?"

"We have apartments for staff here on campus. We can put you in one of those until you can find your own apartment in the city."

"This all sounds amazing, but…"

"No buts, dear. Don't overthink it. If you are interested in the role, if the job excites you and you love the city, then take a chance on it. Live a little. If you don't enjoy it, you can always go back to Seattle. What do you say?"

"I say, I'd love to. Yes, I accept."

"Wonderful news. Can you come to my office today? We can make arrangements for your apartment and a start date."

"Absolutely, I'll leave the airport now and make my way to you."

....

Callum walked across campus as quickly as he could, trying to get to his car as fast as his legs would allow him. Almost running, he finally reached his car and slid behind the wheel. He expertly blended into traffic and made his way to the airport. There was no way he would let Charlotte leave Scotland without at least knowing how he felt about her.

As he got onto the main road, the traffic became denser the closer he got to the airport. He was almost at a standstill, bumper to bumper with the rest of the cars on the road. Why was it when you really needed to get somewhere quickly, traffic was always slower than a snail?

Callum sat in traffic for what felt like forever. He quickly checked his phone every time traffic came to a standstill. Charlotte still hadn't responded to him, he just hoped that she hadn't got on a plane back to Seattle yet. Just as he started to drive again, his phone beeped a message from Bernard, but he was unable to read it while he was driving. He assumed it was just Bernard telling him to let it go and come back to work or wondering why he'd left so quickly.

....

Charlotte grabbed her things and made her way out of the airport terminal. It was a long walk to get from the airport terminal gates to where the taxi cabs waited outside of the airport. Though Charlotte was excited to make her way back into Edinburgh city and to Bernard's office to talk about her future here, she still took her time, enjoying the walk. Her thoughts raced gently in her mind as she made her way to the airport entrance. Maybe she could be with Callum after all, maybe she had a future with him and in Edinburgh. Maybe this would be the place she finally felt at home.

She finally found the entrance to the airport. Stepping into the cold air, she shivered slightly and looked around for the taxicab rank.

....

Callum finally made his way to the airport and parked in the first spot he could find. He made a mental note of the space number he'd parked in and found his way out of the parking deck. As he hurried to the airport entrance, he saw a familiar figure coming out of the main entrance, Charlotte.

He walked up to her as fast as he could, catching her eye as she turned to face his direction.

"Callum….?" Charlotte almost whispered his name, her voice almost in shock.

"Charlotte!" Callum jogged the last few steps between them and caught her in his arms. He twirled her around in his grasp and put her gently back on the ground.

"Callum, what are you doing here?"

"Stopping you from leaving. Please don't go, Charlotte. Stay here with me."

"What about Amelie?"

"Amelie?"

"Yes, aren't you two… you know."

"God no. We work together and we're friends, but we aren't together. Charlotte, Amelie is gay."

"Oh!"

"Please stay, Charlotte."

"Yes, I mean, I was going to stay anyway. Bernard offered me a job at the University, but I'd like to stay even more now that you want me to." Charlotte laughed slightly as she told Callum about her recent job offer.

"You're staying?! For good?" Callum was overjoyed.

"Yes, I just got off the phone with Bernard. I'm actually headed to see him now."

Callum swept Charlotte up in his arms again, this time, as he put her back on the ground, he kissed her passionately.

"Callum…" his name was a groan on her lips. She smiled up at him.

"Charlotte, there's something I never got a chance to tell you."

"Oh?" Her brows furrowed together in confusion.

"I… I love you, Charlotte."

"Oh Callum… I love you too!"

The two stood together for a while, each comforted in each other's embrace, smiling in between kisses.

"Come on, I'll take you to Bernard. But once you get done with him, promise me you'll give me some of your time."

"I'd give you all of my time if I could, Callum."

....

"Ah Charlotte, Callum. I'm so glad you found one another."

"I'll leave you two alone. Charlotte, let me know when you're done, and I'll come and pick you up." Callum gently kissed her forehead, nodded at Bernard and left the room.

"Charlotte, come, take a seat. We have much to discuss about your position."

....

Charlotte was exhausted by the time she'd finished with Bernard. He'd given her information about her new job, they'd filed so much paperwork she'd forgotten her own signature, and he'd given her a small tour of his offices and her new apartment. It was small, but perfect to start her journey in Scotland. They'd spoken for hours about everything and though tiring, Charlotte had never been more excited to start a new job, a new life.

Feeling the need to decompress, Charlotte made her way to a cafe in the city. She sat and cupped her hot cappuccino, happily gazing out of the window and watching passersby.

Her phone buzzed in her pocket. Charlotte reached to answer it. Daisy. She was happy to hear from her friend and spent the next hour telling her all about the job offer and her new apartment. Though disappointed that she wouldn't be seeing her friend soon, Daisy was happy for her friend.

Hanging up the phone, Charlotte dialed Callum.

"Charlotte, are you ready? I can pick you up, we can grab something to eat on the way home."

"Home?"

"My apartment is your home, if you want it to be."

"I'd like that, eventually. Maybe not right now, but someday."

"I suppose I can wait for you." Callum chuckled. Charlotte's heart fluttered as she imagined everything, she ever wanted coming true before her eyes.

"I'm ready, I'm in the town though. At the coffee shop."

"The one where you first bumped into me?"

"Yes, it's becoming my favorite."

"Mine too. I'll be right there. Stay put."

Charlotte finished up her drink as she waited for Callum. She sensed him before she saw him enter the cafe, she felt that she would always sense when he was close. Looking up, their eyes met, and they smiled at each other.

"Ready?" Callum smiled down at her and took her hand.

"For you? Always." As she stood, she wrapped her arms around him, and he kissed her gently.

....

EPILOGUE

Charlotte sipped on her coffee as she sat watching the world go by in the cafe window. It was springtime in Edinburgh, so the hustle and bustle of the city was back to normal, people weren't slowed down by ice and snow. She smiled as she watched people shopping or stopping to look in windows. She loved this city, her home.

"Well, well, well. I knew I'd find you here." Charlotte smiled and looked up to see Callum walking towards her.

"What are you doing here? I didn't think I'd get to see you today." She turned her face up to greet him as he landed a gentle kiss on her lips.

"I have something for you." He slid into the seat opposite her and fished a small box out of his pocket.

"What is it?"

"Open it." Callum grinned as he handed her the box.

She opened it up. Inside was a small cloth bag with a tuppence wrapped up in tissue paper inside it.

"What's this for?"

"It's a tuppence….", Callum looked a little confused at her question.

"No, I see that, but what do I do with it?" It was Charlotte's turn to look confused.

"Oh. The rhyme… something borrowed, something blue, something old, something new… and a tuppence for her shoe. It's for luck, tomorrow." Callum smiled to himself.

"I never knew that rhyme had an ending! I love it, thank you so much."

"I spoke to the girls, they said you had everything else. I wanted to give you the last piece."

"I love it Callum."

"I'd better get going. I just wanted to give you that and sneak in a few extra kisses before the wedding. This time tomorrow, you will be Mrs. Callum McKenzie!"

"I can't wait!"

The two grinned at each other. Charlotte watched as Callum made his way out of the cafe. He gave her one last look, waved and blew her a kiss before exiting the cafe.

Charlotte felt warm inside, like she'd been hugged by a big bear. She was beyond excited for the wedding tomorrow, if not a little nervous! There were lots more she had to do before she went back to the hotel to meet Daisy and Amelie.

Amelie. Charlotte had been so sure she was in a relationship with Callum. Since working at the University, Charlotte had become firm friends with Amelie, and was so happy that she'd agreed to be one of her bridesmaids.

....

"This is it! Are you nervous?" Daisy gently pulled Charlotte's veil out of her eyes and smiled up at her.

"Yes! But mainly I'm excited!" Charlotte's stomach was in knots, her butterflies hadn't settled since she'd got to the venue that morning.

"You got this! Just don't trip!" Amelie laughed as she handed Charlotte her bouquet of flowers.

"You better catch me if I do!"

"We will!" Amelie and Daisy spoke in unison.

"Let's do this ladies!" Daisy grabbed everyone's hands and moved them to position. It was time to marry Callum McKenzie.

....

As Callum and Charlotte said their 'I do's', Callum couldn't help but grin. He had everything he wanted in Charlotte and couldn't wait to start the rest of their lives together.

He kissed her with promise of what was to come, and she smiled up at him.

"I love you, Callum."

"I love you more, Charlotte."

....

Printed in Great Britain
by Amazon

51500750R00113